MW01483987

The Settle Down Society: Book One

The Weekend We Met

a romance

Natalie Keller Reinert

Also by Natalie Keller Reinert

Sorry I Kissed You

The Settle Down Society
The Weekend We Met
The Settle Down Summer
The Business of Fairy Tales (2024)
The Tropical Update (2024)

Catoctin Creek
Sunset at Catoctin Creek
Snowfall at Catoctin Creek
Springtime at Catoctin Creek
Christmas at Catoctin Creek

Ocala Horse Girls
The Project Horse
The Sweetheart Horse
The Regift Horse
The Hollywood Horse

The Florida Equestrian Collection
The Eventing Series
Briar Hill Farm
Grabbing Mane: A Duet
Show Barn Blues: A Duet
Alex & Alexander: A Horse Racing Saga
Sea Horse Ranch: A Beach Read Series
The Hidden Horses of New York: A Novel

Theme Park Adventures
You Must Be This Tall
Confessions of a Theme Park Princess

Chapter One

My name is Maeve Benson, and I only know that because I wrote it down.

No, no, that's not true. I'm joking! Things can get pretty dire, but they're not *that* bad.

Just in case, though, my name is written in my notebook. Along with my phone number, of course. Because I'd be lost if anything should happen to it. There's certainly no way I'd remember where I'd left it.

It's open in front of me just now, while I scribble some notes about the morning into it.

Cappuccino, extra foam, two brown sugars and a chocolate drop. I finger the foil wrapper left crumpled on the saucer. *Something Italian. Nice touch. A+ for Margot today.*

I do love a good cup of coffee. Cafe & Croissant is half the reason I moved to West Eighty-first Street in the first place. You need a good cafe for the commute in this city, and this little French-themed coffee shop is halfway between my studio apartment and the low-slung brick building in Central Park where I clock in and out each day. And it's such a perfect place: cozy, intimate, quiet...

"Hey, imagine meeting you here!"

Well, it's *usually* quiet. But this male voice which just boomed a greeting is causing a reaction that ripples across the entire cafe like a seismic wave. I jump and look up, startled, along with just about everyone else in the little room.

We've all had the same reaction, as we look up from our Saturday morning muffins and mugs: mostly surprised, somewhat annoyed. I'm prepared to give the subject of that overly enthusiastic greeting a sympathetic look. I hate to see people embarrassed in public. Only, who is she? Who was that loud voice talking to? No one looks like the guilty party.

In fact, everyone is looking from the man to—to *me*.

And actually, he's looking at me, too. With a wide, happy grin on his face. "Just kidding," he says, "I knew you'd be here!"

Oh, no.

With a sense of doom, I realize what is happening. This isn't a case of mistaken identity—some random thinking I'm some girl he met in a club late at night, or a missed connection from a subway station downtown.

I've forgotten someone.

It doesn't happen very often, because I am careful—witness the notebook! And I try to avoid meeting too many strangers, which is a nice way of saying I don't go out of my way to make friends...or date...so that situations like this don't come up more than they have to.

But Manhattan is basically a village, especially when you take individual neighborhoods into account. Life often takes place within the same square six or seven blocks, and you keep bumping into the same people over and over. Maybe you find yourself walking past a friend's former roommate in the hallway, or some lady you always stand behind at the salad place on Broadway starts saying hello to you, so eventually the two of you begin chatting in line like you are actual friends.

You *aren't* friends with that lady, obviously. Just two people thrown together in the crazy churn of this city. But you feel like you can share a salad-related conversation for five minutes, even if you have nothing else in common. It's harmless. For most people.

For me, it's a little different. If my friend's ex-roommate or the lady from the salad place run into me out of context, like on a street corner or waiting for the subway...or, yes, sitting in some quiet French cafe, they'll remember me.

But I won't remember them.

My cheeks redden as a tall, lean man I don't recognize slides into the chair across from me. He places broad hands on the pale finish of the table, spreading them out like starfish, and announces, in the same loud voice as before, "I can't believe you're here right now! Let me buy you a muffin."

With this friendly offer extended, he smiles at me winningly. He seems so nice.

Honestly, if he wasn't so loud, this wouldn't be so awkward.

Oh, and if he wasn't a total stranger to me. There is that.

The usual questions crowd my brain: who is this guy, and where have I met him before? Waiting on line at the bank, tripping over my own shoelaces on the sidewalk, fumbling with my key outside my building?

He's pretty hot, so I have to admit there's some real incentive here to figure out if I've actually met him.

So, instead of getting up and running away screaming about stranger danger, I give this loud man a weak smile in return while I run my eyes over his face, looking for any saving signature to jog my memory, to remind me where and when we've met before.

My memory basically works; it's my *recall* that's broken. That's why my note-taking system usually works for me. If I can find the right entry in my notebooks, it can all come back to me. Occasionally, failing easy access to my notes, I can latch onto some particular feature of a face or a place, and my memory will spark to life.

But, so far, this guy isn't starting any fires. And that's too bad, because he seems like the kind of man I'd like to know better.

I love his looks: soft, brown hair which wants to flop into his eyes, which are hazel and seem kind. He has a high forehead and a strong nose, a cleft chin and just a hint of a morning shadow, but nothing like a beard. To put things succinctly, he is a tall, wide-shouldered, plain t-shirt wearing guy...like a thousand others in this quiet Upper West Side neighborhood.

That makes it difficult. I could have met him anywhere between my apartment and work. I could have met him while I was working, or maybe even right here, in this quiet cafe where I stop every morning, Monday through Saturday, for caffeine and kind baristas and the illusion of company in my semi-isolated life.

Finally, I venture, "How did you know I'd be here?"

Hopefully we didn't make plans.

"I remembered you saying you liked the muffins here," he says. His voice is still a couple of decibels too loud. People are shuffling their things on their tables, murmuring. He doesn't seem to notice. Maybe he's hard of hearing. Would we have talked about that? "Blueberry, right? Or was it something exotic? Huckleberry? I forget. Anyway, you said you always come on Saturday morning to read for a while. And here you are!"

His smile is so wide, it's as if he conjured me up with sheer enthusiasm.

No, I couldn't have met him here at the cafe. He's far too loud and everyone's response is too memorable. I might not remember most things I didn't write down, but I'd sure recall being embarrassed enough to want to drop through the floor of Cafe & Croissant.

"Let me get you a muffin," he says, glancing towards the bakery case next to the cash register. Margot is leaning over the counter, red lips parted with avid curiosity while she watches the two of us.

"Thank you, but no muffins for me today," I say apologetically. "I had a breakfast burrito before I came. Still stuffed."

"Oh, man, I love a breakfast burrito! From Tortilla Jo's? I just discovered that place and it's great. Have you been?" His eyes light up with the discovery that we both love burritos.

He's so *eager*. It makes me feel terrible about not remembering him. His feelings would be so hurt if he found out. If I could just get a second alone to flip through my notebook! He's gotta be in here...

"Actually, I make homemade burritos," I answer, twisting the foil from my chocolate drop into a little ball. "I like them with green chiles, which are hard to get fresh here—"

"Right, because you're from New Mexico!" he exclaims, thrilled with himself. His voice is basically shaking the vintage chandelier hanging over our heads. Great, now I'm worried we'll be crushed by a heavy brass light fixture. "Now, I remember. *That's* where I got huckleberry from. You said you can only get huckleberry muffins back in Albuquerque, right?"

Wait, that's actually correct and *very* specific.

I stare at him, utterly confused. He beams right back at me, his hazel eyes sparkling with glints of gold in the morning light.

This guy and I definitely shared some kind of conversation. Seems like we'd hit it off, too. So why can't I remember him yet?

I *have* to check my notes. I can't just blow this guy off; even he if didn't seem immune to brush-offs, he's nice. He knows about me.

I want to know more about him.

I push back my chair, saying, "Can you excuse me for a minute? I'll be *right* back."

"Yeah, of course. I was going to get a coffee anyway, so I'll just..." He gestures with his head towards the counter, where Margot has straightened up and is reading what appears to be a handmade 'zine. Her long, white-blonde hair is slipping free of its braid; a thick lock falls over her face and she shakes it back impatiently.

I know the 'zine is just a prop to make it look like she hasn't been watching everything go down with me and the Loudest Man in New York.

Margot has been working weekend mornings here for a few months, to save money for an art project she's been planning for a community garden on the Lower East Side. I was thrilled when she decided to get a job at my cafe, because Margot is one of my closest friends. And the truth is, she'd probably know if I'd met a nice, noisy, brown-haired, hazel-eyed guy with a cleft in his chin and shoulders so wide he could probably carry me around on them.

After all, I probably would have met him here and even if I hadn't, I'd have told her about him over my Saturday morning coffee.

I have a routine; I find routines are good for me. This cafe is the core of my morning, the best and most certain way I keep track of my life.

It goes like this:

I stop in to Cafe & Croissant every morning on my way to the park, at about six thirty. Just when the opening barista sleepily unlocks the front door. Few people have to get to the subway or into a car for work so early, so the cafe is always quiet, often only half-lit. I like to sit down with my current notebook —this month, it's red. I sip at whatever Margot or one of her coworkers feels like making me—they like to see their work reviewed in my little jottings for the day—and read over the day before, to lock the memories into place with as much glue as my synapses could offer.

I usually stay until just after seven, then walk the rest of the way to work.

I *have* met people on these quiet, early mornings in the cafe. Interesting people, on their way to work or the airport, or on their way home from a late night out. I write down their details after they leave, just in case. But I rarely meet them again.

Or I maybe I do meet them again, but I don't realize it. If that's the case, it's probably because they don't generally sit across from me and offer to buy me breakfast. That, I should remember.

I'd absolutely write it down. In detail.

The mystery man is up at the counter now, talking to Margot. His voice has dropped to a normal, inside voice. She glances at me and winks, then looks back at the man. He's talking earnestly. She laughs and touches his arm.

Whoa, what?

A little wisp of jealousy unfurls in my stomach.

But in the next moment, she's shaking her head at him, rolling her eyes at whatever he's just said. They seem like friends.

What am I missing? I need answers, now. I scoop my notebook into my leather satchel, slide the strap over my arm, and slink off to the restroom. Judging by the growing buzz of families in the cafe, I'll have about three minutes to flip through the past few weeks of my notebook and figure out if I've recently met a loud, handsome, charming man, before someone starts knocking impatiently.

Will it be enough time to save me from another awkward interaction? I could only hope. He seems really nice. I *want* to know him, I realize, as I lock the bathroom door.

I want him to be someone I've already met, someone I can get to know better.

I want to remember him.

Chapter Two

NOTHING. *NOTHING.* MY allotted three minutes have come and gone, and there is definitely a creak to the floorboards just outside the restroom door, which means pretty soon someone is going to get fed up waiting and either knock or try the vintage glass doorknob. I can just imagine some tired mother in tasteful knits bursting in with her paranoid parental brain expecting some kind of medical emergency, only to see me leaning over the porcelain sink, flipping frantically through a cherry-red notebook.

She'll probably scold me with the door hanging open behind her, while everyone in the cafe is watching avidly. So far, I've found these Upper West Side moms are not afraid to dress down any twenty-somethings they find who insist on living in their midst without fulfilling the local requirement to get married and produce a child. They moved here from much cooler neighborhoods in order to raise their families and it's my job to do the same.

And if I won't produce, I better be a good example to their youngsters.

Just last week, an exhausted-looking woman with three children toting unridden scooters gave me a scathing reminder to wait for the green before crossing the street. "Don't be a bad example to the children in this neighborhood!" she'd snapped, pointing back at her three astonished angels.

Margot tells me I'm crazy to live up here in Wealthy Family Central, but what can I say? I work in Central Park and I like walking to the office.

The floorboard just outside makes an ominous groan. Yup, someone is *definitely* pacing out there. I'm out of time for this particular bathroom. And as far as I can tell, there's nothing in this notebook about meeting a nice brown-haired, hazel-eyed man with broad shoulders and a disturbing lack of volume control.

But, how? How could there be nothing? Why wouldn't I have written something about meeting a nice man whose eyes give me a warm feeling? They aren't exactly common.

And to think, we'd had a real chat. Apparently, we'd talked about huckleberries and hometowns! That kind of conversation would have *meant* something to me. I don't go around discussing my private details with just anyone.

I barely discuss my private life with my friends, for heaven's sake. I keep my cards close to my chest. Safer, that way.

But somehow this guy nabbed my details and escaped before I could write it all down.

It's all so unlike me.

At least, I think it is.

There is always a chance I do this kind of thing on the regular and just...forget.

Sighing, I close the notebook and give myself one long look in the speckled mirror, memorizing my features as if I'm a stranger to myself. My memory issues don't extend that far, thank goodness. And my face, luckily, hasn't changed much in my mid-twenties. Or maybe unluckily? Depends on your perspective, I guess. Probably, a lot of women hoped for more from the looks lottery than curly nut-brown hair, chestnut eyes to match, and skin which tans so readily, my landscaping job keeps me looking like I've just gotten back from a month in Aruba.

But my dad has always said, with such fondness, how much I look like his mother—minus the tan of course, as she was Irish, straight out of County Clare—and I'd learned at an early age how important memories could be.

I don't mind reminding him of someone else he loves. Reminders of good things are far too few in this life.

A certain nice-looking, broad-shouldered, loud-voiced, warm-feeling-inducing man outside this room being my case in point.

There is a tentative knock at the door.

I have officially overstayed my welcome.

I drop my notebook back into my bag and eye the narrow window over the alley for one foolish moment. No. This isn't a sitcom, and I have to accept my fate. Which will be sheer embarrassment, as I explain to him that I really didn't remember him, and request that he refresh my memory on where we first met.

It will be awful, of course; he'll feel foolish and men hate feeling foolish in front of women. He'll make his excuses and head out the door and that will be that. He'll find a new cafe. There are plenty in this neighborhood. No shortage of caffeine infusions and French pastry when the average household income is six figures and up.

I open the door, step around the impatient woman outside without bothering to make eye contact, and head back to my table.

He isn't there.

I glance back at the counter, looking for him.

Margot is dropping coins into the register, her annoyed "I can't believe I have to handle cash" expression on her face.

She's alone.

My eyes rove over the cafe. He's the type that stands out in a place like this. He's like a—what is that evocative expression I read recently, in a sweet old Scottish novel—oh, right! A bison in a bun shop. That is the perfect expression for him. He's too big for New York City. Too full for Manhattan's narrow aisles and tiny spaces. Too loud to stay anonymous in a packed room.

Once again, I think, I *should* remember this guy.

Margot closes the register drawer with a sigh and looks up.

Our gazes meet.

A twinkle immediately sparkles in her bold blue eyes. She glances around for potential customers, then darts around the counter. In a flash of red and blue—Margot loves bright clothes, and her weekday job teaching art to Lower Manhattan kids inspires her to buy lots of primary colors—she's sitting across from me.

"Well, we *love* that he's back," she purrs.

"Do we?" So, Margot does know him! "He's kind of loud, huh?"

"He's *very* loud. But I told him he needed to keep his voice down and he managed just fine. He said he'd been coaching youth baseball this morning, down at the park, and he just gets used to shouting."

A youth baseball coach? In the park? Oh, so maybe I *did* meet him at work. Not that a gardener like me spends much time on baseball diamonds, but we could have come across each other on a Central Park path. I feel a little tingle of excitement. We still have a shot. We can still figure this out.

My weak smile is turning into a grin as I ask Margot, "Okay, so where did Mr. Baseball go?"

"Home, to get his dog out for a walk," she replies, lazily running a towel over the counter. "But he asked me to tell you not to be mad that he hasn't called since he got back. He said he had his phone stolen on the D train, like the *minute* he got back into the city, and he was so embarrassed about it." Margot laughs. "What a dork. I said he better not stand too close to the doors with his phone out next time. I mean, we've told him before that he would have to toughen up if he wanted to make it in this town!"

Wait, what? *We've told him before?*

*We...*meaning Margot and me?

Or were other people around when we met, too?

Oh, this is the worst feeling! I hate this. It's why I don't meet people if I can help it.

Margot is moving on already, flicking her pink fingernails at my notebook. "Writing your poems?"

Everyone likes to guess what I write in my notebooks. Margot thinks I am a secret poet. I let her believe it. Why not? Better than the truth.

"That's right." I tug the notebook closer to me and Margot laughs.

"So secretive! Don't worry. I'd never steal your verses, darling."

The bell on the door jingles and Margot looks up, sighing at the idea of more work. A family of five, with scooters in tow, comes tramping into the cafe. She glances at the register to check the time.

"Ten o'clock already! It's all parents with kids from here on out," she groused. "Summer weekend shifts are hell, did you know that? Frappes until my fingers bleed. Whipped cream and sprinkles everywhere. I love kids, but only when there isn't a lot of sugar involved. The kids at my school aren't allowed sugar. Or wheat. Can you imagine? They'd never survive back on the farm. Speaking of kids, though, before you go—"

She eyeballs the mother of the family, who is already standing about six inches behind me. "Are you going to do the garden half of my summer mural project? We meet with the board next weekend to get final approval on the design."

I hesitate, hating myself for not agreeing immediately. But I have my reasons for avoiding a community arts project. Children have soft feelings. I don't want to wound any of them.

"Come on," Margot urges. "I could *really* use your help. The mural is great, obviously, but without the garden component it loses some of its punch."

"I wish I could," I begin, dropping my gaze to the floor. "But —"

"But you won't." Margot sighs. "Come on, why not? It's just Saturday afternoons for like, six weeks. Hardly anything. And you'd be doing me, your awesome friend, a huge favor. Plus getting all kinds of brownie points with the city for volunteering. It could take you to the next level at work!"

"There is no next level in my job," I lie. "It's just gardening. Hands in the dirt." As if there aren't landscape architect positions I would love to apply for. But I'm still miles down the seniority list. City jobs are a long game. Some people put in a decade before they move up. I've been there less than a year. "I'm really sorry, but there's no way I can fit it in."

"Ahem," coughs the mother behind me, and the wheel of a scooter goes crashing into my ankle.

I press my lips together, holding back some very un-family language. "I wish I could," I say at last. "I'll talk to you later, okay? Pizza tonight?"

"You got it, babe," Margot says, evidently forgiving me. "Don't know how we'd live without our Saturday night pizzas. It's how I remember who I am."

Chapter Three

I'M NOT THE kind of person who avoids my workplace on my days off. After all, I work for the city parks department, so if I avoid my "office" all weekend, I'm really only hurting myself. I especially like visiting my park on the weekend. I love the differences between weekdays and weekends.

The way the pace slows on the sidewalks, all that rushing to work slowed to something more like an amble—or as close to an amble as a New Yorker can manage.

The way summer clothes brighten up the paths, somber office blacks traded for leggings and sundresses and brightly printed madras shorts.

The way the park meadows and greens go from quiet seas of grass to party headquarters inundated with happy locals and starstruck tourists stretched out on beach towels, playing Frisbee, eating lavish picnics, and napping in the sun.

I love that Central Park is an oasis for everyone, a people's paradise of greenery, and even more, I love that I have a hand in making it beautiful and welcoming. When I chose a vocational program in landscaping over traditional college, I got a lot of pushback from friends and family, even my high school teachers who knew how much I loved my gardens. But I knew that working with plants was the right path for me, and not just because gardening was an orderly and solitary affair which meshed well with my memory's shortcomings.

Plants never ask what I think of them, and they don't expect me to remember birthdays, they just respond to my attention by growing.

I appreciate that kind of distance in a coworker. No one asking questions, no one delving too deep into my personal life. I have my secrets, and I don't know any other way to live.

Moreover, planting gardens is an act of giving which makes me happy. When I dig up dirt and lay out a beautiful garden, I am *giving* something to the world: beauty, nourishment, even a new source of fresh air. In a place like Manhattan, this is a gift my fellow residents sorely need.

So Monday through Friday, from seven in the morning to three thirty in the afternoon, I plant gardens for the people of New York City.

And on Saturday morning, around ten o'clock, I wander through my gardens and watch the people enjoy them.

Over the past week, I've been laboring over a planting project outside the Delacorte Theater. The summer season's annual Shakespeare in the Park performances are about to begin, and the outdoor amphitheater will become a focal point of the city's social calendar. I've been working in the Shakespeare Garden since spring, and my boss decided I've earned the right to design the fenced green near the entrance. It's a big break for me. Despite my earlier assertion that I have no shot at a promotion, I do want to design my own gardens, not just plant what I'm told.

So I was over the moon when Lara told me the Delacorte project was mine.

I planted bright borders and tall, colorful blooms, something to draw patrons' eyes while they waited in the final stretch of the long, long lines to get in. With my prior experience working on the Shakespeare Garden, I was able to pull together an English country garden straight out of an Anglophile's dream. All it is missing now is a tea service and a red phone booth.

I finished the garden yesterday, and today I want to see my blooms in action. It's below the Eighty-sixth Street entrance, so I cross Central Park West amidst the crowds of tourists outside the Museum of Natural History, wave to the hot dog vendors on either corner, and amble down the sidewalk beneath the cover of trees in their thick green summer crowns.

The theater is just a short distance away, and I can already see the riot of color well before I draw near. I have to smile at what I see: the garden is getting plenty of attention. There are a few couples taking selfies with the hollyhocks reaching high behind them, and a young woman leaning over the fence, taking close-up pictures of a bee luxuriating in a pollen-filled coneflower.

Despite the buzzing activity on the walkways, the constant bicycles whizzing past, and the sound of traffic from Central Park West, the scene around the garden is quiet, peaceful, even inspirational—everything I was hoping for. This is about to become a bustling box office location in just a few days, but there will be calming vibes from the garden.

"This place is like heaven," I hear a woman murmur, and she strolls over to admire the flowers with her partner's hand in hers. They look like they've stepped right out of a rom-com. All I need now is Meg Ryan to come around the corner and bump into Tom Hanks, and I'll be in Nora Ephron heaven.

I did this, I think with elation. *I made this happiness!*

"Hey, Maeve!"

That voice. That too-loud, so friendly, voice. He's here! At *my* garden!

I can feel a prickle of excitement which starts in my tailbone and runs all the way up my back, so fast I can't even quench it with a cold bucket of common sense.

I try, though. There are lots of reasons to run into him here.

Of course, he's come to the park; Margot said he'd be walking his dog. Of course, he's walked up the West Drive; it's the closest section to the West 80s—where he probably lives, since he was just at Cafe & Croissant.

It's not *fate* or anything.

I deliberately don't turn around. I'll just be cool, I'll just let him tap me on the shoulder and I'll be like, 'Whoa, surprise seeing you again so soon.' A real ice-cold character, that's me—

"Maeve, over here!"

I just can't resist the infectious happiness in his voice. I whirl around, and there he is—being led by a lanky black Labrador with a red collar and a goofy expression. I can't decide which of them is cuter. I mean, obviously they're cute in different ways. He's so broad-shouldered and his face is so open and giving... but the dog really is adorable. Like, get down on your knees and kiss her nose, adorable.

"Hey, Maeve, look at us meeting up again! I was just walking my dog."

You see? He's just walking his dog! Not meeting you at your garden like you had some kind of prior assignation all set up.

But Central Park is so big, I remind the naysaying voice in my head. He could have gone anywhere else and been miles away from me. He might have turned south, or gone across to the east side, or entered on the north side and wandered in the wood. There's actually almost no chance we'd just randomly run into each other here, when you look at it like that. Cold, hard facts.

Then again, if he's here at my most recent project, maybe this is where we met. Maybe he was hoping I'd come back here and he'd see me.

Maybe I'd even agreed to meet him here!

I *had* been really focused on this project, and I didn't usually have time to make notes while I was working...

It's possible meeting him simply slipped my mind because I'd been so intent on my garden.

That *must* be it, I decide. We met here, while I was gardening. Mystery solved.

It doesn't explain how he knows Margot.

Either way, I'm accepting the win. I like this guy, he has a dog, and he's here in my favorite place in the world. So I paste a smile on my face and hold out my hand for his excited dog to sniff.

"You again," I tell him, foolishly. "Imagine that!"

"Me again," he agrees, equally silly. "Say hi to Bashful! Bashful, this is Maeve!"

The dog wags her tail so hard it looks like her entire back end is going to come loose and go skidding across the sidewalk. She licks my hand with sloppy enthusiasm.

"Bashful," I repeat in a neutral tone. I'm conflicted about the name but don't want to question it, in case he has already told me about his dog's weird name. Nothing says, 'Hi, I forgot we ever met before this,' quite like repeating entire conversations.

"I know, it's so silly," he laughs. He has a nice laugh—not too loud, after all. Not as noisy as I first thought. But then again, maybe I thought the same thing the *first* time we'd met. "My niece named her...she found some Snow White book that her mom had in a box, the kind with a cassette tape that reads the book to you, from like a hundred years ago? And she made my sister get a tape player and everything. So now every day is all Snow White, all the time, and all the animals she meets get named for different dwarves."

I burst into surprised laughter. That is so *cute!* Little nieces with hand-me-down tape players. Is he kidding me? I love it. "She's a future hipster. They're all going to be carrying around tape players and vintage audiobooks in twenty years. I guess it's a good thing she didn't name this lovely girl Grumpy, huh?"

"Oh, that name would not fit." He gazes at his dog fondly. "Although I admit Bashful isn't too accurate, either."

Bashful transfers her attentions from me to a fresh audience as a group of tourists spot her and begin cooing with delight.

"Well, I'm forgotten," I chuckle, as she dances around the tourists' feet, tongue lolling. "Chopped liver."

"Except she'd love chopped liver," he informs me, eyes sparkling. "Because dogs are disgusting. Listen, you want to go for a walk with us? I usually give her a couple of miles on Saturday to really wear her out, and we've only walked up from Heckscher Ballfields. She hasn't even begun to feel it yet. I'm thinking Turtle Pond, then some hills in The Ramble, maybe a hot dog at Bethesda Terrace for lunch? Since I couldn't stick around and buy you that muffin, of course. You interested?"

I make myself hesitate, think it over, even though my heart leaps—and leaps unaccountably high, I have to say—at his invitation. I would *love* to go on a walk with this very nice man and his very rowdy dog.

And figure out how I know him. And his name. Ugh, his *name!* This could get awkward. I should have just asked Margot...

"I'll buy the hot dogs," he adds, misreading my hesitation. "In case that wasn't absolutely clear."

He's charming. I'll give him that. He's terribly charming.

And there's nothing quite like a Central Park hot dog after a good long walk.

My mind has clearly made itself up. After all, what's the worst that can happen? Even if he turns out to be a serial killer (always a possibility) there isn't much he can do right now. This is a stroll through one of the busiest parks in the world, on a sunny summer day, and I know everyone who works here, besides. I'll just be sure to say hello to everyone I see, and he'll understand there are too many witnesses to risk murdering me. Problem solved.

One problem, anyway.

"Well, in *that* case," I tell him, grinning. "Thanks for clarifying. I would love to go on a walk with you and Bashful."

His face lights up. He has such a nice smile. There is no way a guy with this kind of bright smile is anything but on the up-and-up. I need to believe this all makes perfect sense—why shouldn't he want to take a walk with me, the nice gardening girl he met in the park? I must have made quite an impression on him. Is that so surprising? I'm pretty impressive.

If you like unruly brown hair and un-manicured nails that sometimes have a little dirt under them, and I believe some people *do* like those things.

"Excellent." He beams down at me, a total ray of sunlight. "Well, Bashful is already pulling us toward Turtle Pond. Shall we go find the turtles?"

"Wouldn't want to keep Bashful waiting!" I agree. As she tugs at the leash, I notice something glimmering on her collar. Ah-hah! I hold up a hand, saying, "Oh, let me just get this leaf off her chest."

I drop to my knees beside Bashful, who pants happily in my ear as I brush a nonexistent leaf away. In the same motion, I twist the heart-shaped tag on her collar around and read the engraved words.

Bashful

IF FOUND: DANE MANSFIELD

There's a phone number, too, but that isn't important right now.

His name is Dane! I love that name.

I stand up again, and Dane smiles at me like he appreciates a woman who will brush off his dog. "You ready now?" he asks.

"Ready," I assure him, then turn in surprise as a child's excited shriek pierces the air around us.

"Mommy, look at those flowers! *Look,* Mommy!" A little girl in a pink princess costume runs past us, her face lit with excitement. She jumps right onto the cast-iron fence and grips the railings, peering into my garden with rapture. "Oh, Mommy, it's *beautiful.*"

I can't help but hang back and watch her for a moment, my heart full.

"Coming?" Dane calls from a few feet down the path. "Bashful is leaving without us." The dog is straining at the leash, ready to continue on her walk.

I glance back at my garden as we stroll away together. He didn't say anything about it. If we'd met here, while I was working on it, wouldn't he at *least* have commented on a job well done?

Somewhere else, then. Maybe as we walk, it will come back to me.

Chapter Four

By the time we reach the wooded entrance to the Ramble, my stomach is growling and I've forgotten to worry about where Dane and I might have met. This guy knows how to take a serious walk. And he wasn't lying when he said Bashful needed to wander for hours on her Saturday morning strolls.

First it was to the Turtle Pond, then a climb up the staircase to Belvedere Castle, the cartoonish stone palace overlooking the park. Here, Bashful noses a startled rat from between some loose rocks, causing some small children to shriek with excitement while their parents rush to grab their hands and drag them away. The rat dives off the castle battlements and into the brush below.

"Impressive!" I tell her. "You're like a real medieval hound up here, Bashful."

Dane looks a little embarrassed. "I told her to save that trick for when we knew each other a little better," he quips. "She's always bringing out the rats before anyone's ready for them."

"I guess she figured we know each other well enough now," I say, rubbing Bashful's lovely black ears. And I don't just mean the dog.

By now, I already feel like I know Dane, in that comfortable way some people just click. His personality is open and outgoing; by nature, he seems kind and giving. He makes way for climbing toddlers when we're climbing stairs; he glances anxiously after elderly people when we're walking on uneven ground. He's a man who looks out for other people. In this city, it's hard to imagine a soul more refreshing.

I encourage him to talk about himself as we follow the path back down to ground level, tugging Bashful past fallen ice cream cones melting into the pavement and squirrels digging into the turf for dropped peanuts. I ask about his morning coaching baseball and he gets very animated talking about his team, the Amsterdam Sluggers. Apparently, everyone is under ten and they are very adorable in their short pants and tall socks.

He's full of stories about the kids. So I find out that Caleb Rubenstein got so hot at a game last weekend that he up-ended an Italian ice in his pants, with ruinous results, while Rooney Linden has a habit of bursting into tears every time he hits the ball.

"But we're working on it," Dane concludes cheerfully, "and we get a lot of practice, because the kid is talented as hell. Eventually he'll dry up."

"Did you play baseball as a kid?" I ask, fingers crossed it hasn't come up before.

"I did! And it was not as fun as this. We were way too serious about our sports back in Indiana." He laughs and draws Bashful back from an abandoned Coke can. "Man, the park is a little messy this morning."

"The weekend crew is probably short-staffed," I say automatically. They are always short-staffed. "And these summer crowds are hard to keep up with."

Indiana, I'm thinking, wishing I could jot it down. *He's from Indiana and he played youth baseball. Remember that!*

"You know a lot about the park operations?" Dane glances over at me, surprised.

"Well, yeah, I—" So he *definitely* didn't meet me here. Dammit. "I work here."

"You *work* here? Maeve, that's great! I knew you wanted to work with plants. I'm so glad it worked out for you!"

I stop walking and stare at him. It takes him two strides to realize I'm not next to him anymore; he manages to stop the marauding Bashful three strides later. We stand in the center of the path, tourists filtering around us as they walk in and out of the wooded labyrinth of trails called The Ramble. A dozen languages filter through the muggy air.

This is the moment where I say to him, *I'm so sorry, but how do we know each other?*

This is the moment where I admit, *I have a weird memory condition. It's from a fall when I was a little kid.*

And next will be the moment where he thinks, *This is too much for me.*

I don't want this walk to end. I don't want this guy to disappear.

I don't want my morning with Dane to collapse the way so many others have. Don't want to read through another notebook entry that says, *Had a nice time, don't think he's going to call.*

I've made this mistake before, and that's the reason why my New York friends don't know what I wrote in my notebooks. It will be the reason Dane doesn't know, either.

So, I swallow back my confession, and smile, and lightly say, "Whoops, can we sit down for a minute? My—um—ankle—"

Nothing like inventing a turned ankle, Jane Austen-style, to change the subject.

"Of course!" Dane leaps into action, all apologies. He closes the distance between us in two quick steps and wraps an arm around me, ushering me to a park bench while his linebacker shoulders clear the pathway of heedless, confused tourists. In a moment I am seated on a bench, feeling hot and dazed with the intensity of his reaction.

And the reassuring pressure of his arm around my shoulders.

Then he draws back, placing one hand on Bashful's head and one on his knee. I miss his strong grip immediately.

He says, "Sorry about that. I didn't see—did you trip?"

"I tripped," I agree. "And, I—um—I stepped on a stick. Silly shoes," I add with a shaky chuckle, kicking up one Converse-clad foot to show him.

"Thin soles," he says. "Gotta be careful. Do you think you hurt yourself? I could try to find some help—"

"I'm fine," I assure him. "I just need a minute. To—"

To recover. To think. To breathe.

"To get over it," I finish lamely.

I take longer than I need, because I've picked a nice spot to have a pretend injury. Water patters cheerfully over stones in a nearby stream, and a pair of cardinals are chirping with their sweet little voices in the overhanging trees. Sure, tourists with selfie sticks and locals with pained expressions choke the walkway, but here on our bench we're safe from all that. Dane is warm and solid next to me, a wall against the chaos of the summer's day, and suddenly I wish today could be a weekday and the paths could be deserted. A park just for the two of us.

And Bashful, of course.

"Feel any better?" Dane asks eventually. "I hear hot dogs are really good for sore feet and turned ankles, actually."

"Oh, really? Because I heard the chopped onions are what really does it."

He wrinkles his nose. "Please tell me you're going to get sauerkraut, like a real red-blooded American."

Time to drop the bombshell. "Dane, I don't know how to say this, but...I *hate* sauerkraut."

He puts his hand over his heart. "Mortally wounded."

"So this is the end of our walk, then." I give him a big cartoon frown. "I understand."

"It was nice while it lasted." Dane stands up and stretches elaborately, nearly elbowing a selfie-stick right out of a tourist's hands. "Bashful, come on. We can't let this pretty lady break our hearts anymore than she already has."

Bashful puts her head in my lap and wags her tail. Her brown eyes gaze up at me with limpid, doggy love. "Dane," I laugh, "did you *teach* her this?"

"I taught her all of this," he says gravely. "You know I'm amazing with dogs, but did you know I was this good?"

You know I'm amazing with dogs.

Do I? Did I? Had this come up before?

"Oh, *fine*," I sigh. "I'll tolerate your sauerkraut if you can tolerate my chopped onions."

"Well, sure, I guess," Dane agrees, smiling like he's won a bet. "I just hope you have mints, in case we kiss."

Chapter Five

MARGOT IS IN the kitchen when I arrive at the place she shares with Tracey in the Lower East Side.

"Kitchen" is a grand term to use for the space, considering the layout of the tiny one-bedroom apartment. It's basically a living room with one wall of cabinets, a fridge, a two-burner stovetop, and a microwave. They added a rolling kitchen island to divide the living room area from the kitchen area, and Margot has a tendency to lean over it and shout, "I'm sorry, I can't hear you while I'm in the other room!" any time we are trying to have a conversation with her from the sofa, which is two feet away.

"Help yourself to booze!" she announces as I close the door behind me, leaving the rattling chains and deadbolts unlocked —they're only used overnight, anyway. "Tracey went to get the pizzas. Abel is late, as usual. And Caitlyn is bringing California rolls because she's being vegetarian again." Margot rolls her eyes.

"But that's good news!" I remind her. Caitlyn's vegetarian kicks are entirely based on economics. When she can afford fancy plant-based meat alternatives and organic produce, she goes full veggie. When she is strapped for cash, it's back to picking through the almost-expired cuts of meat at the seedier grocery stores. Lately, she's been interning at a small television station in Jamaica, Queens and the pay isn't good. The pay is a Metrocard, actually. They cover her commute and nothing else. But they let her go on-air and Caitlyn's dream is to actually cover the news, live and in person.

She must have gotten a side project that is paying her in cash if she can afford to go meatless this week. Or maybe she even got a promotion.

"I guess you're right," Margot agrees, setting a six-pack of Coke next to a bottle of Jack Daniels. "I like Caitlyn well-fed. But if she gets preachy about pepperoni being murder, she's going to have to go back to being poor or get out of my apartment."

Margot is from Iowa and her parents raise corn, cattle, and pigs. She is very adamant that meat is delicious. Tracey is from her same tiny farming town, but her mother owns a yarn shop, so she's less militant about meat consumption.

Their small-town backgrounds are one of the many things I have in common with Margot and Tracey—and their college friend Abel, who is part of our little group. Yes, they'd gone to a tiny art school in a small Midwestern town bursting with Greek revival architecture, and I'd gone to an Albuquerque vocational school partially housed in a strip mall, but we both came from practical, sturdy stock: people who did their chores without complaining, shrugged off disasters, and always looked for the best in others. When I came to the city last August, I somehow ended up in their circle and fit perfectly—I'm still not sure how we all ended up friends, but life had been such a haze during those first few chaotic weeks, I couldn't come close to documenting it all.

However it happened, we've been close ever since. Some things you just don't question.

Our Saturday night pizza feast is one of the ways we keep connected, even when city life and careers are making us crazy. Margot is always busy with her community art projects outside of teaching and making coffee; Tracey has a demanding job at an art gallery with lots of late night parties; Abel is writing for an art blog that sends him all over the five boroughs. And of course, now I live on the other side of the city and hardly ever leave my neighborhood. Without a standing date holding us together, we might accidentally drift apart.

I'm always grateful for the effort we collectively put into our friendship, even if I don't remember when it all began.

I pour myself a drink and flop onto the big blue couch which takes up most of the living room. The door to the single bedroom, divided down the middle with a temporary (and illegal) wall, is hanging open. Margot's unmade twin bed is heaped with clothes, as usual, while Tracey's tidy bed looks as if she is practicing for a future vocation as a nun. "Looks like you hit the thrift stores hard this afternoon," I comment. "New stuff?"

"Got some good tips from some customers after you left and decided to go wild," Margot says, settling down next to me. "Some stuff to keep, some to sell. These old guys never know what they've really got on those racks. I've made five hundred bucks in the past two months alone reselling stuff. I'd feel bad if it wasn't for a good cause."

"It all goes back into the mural project, right?"

"Yup. The community board can only spare so much. I needed two grand to get it off the ground, and I crossed that line last week. So, I'm getting a little more ambitious." She takes out her phone. "I was working on some new ideas for the garden, look here—"

I'm bracing myself to tell Margot, once and for all, that I can't work on the garden with her. But Tracey saves me, swinging the door open with one foot. Her tiny frame is laden with pizza boxes. Behind her, Abel looms, holding up two six-packs of hard seltzer. He looks like a mountain behind a seashell.

"I brought booze!" he cries.

Tracey rolls her eyes as she sets the pizzas on the kitchen island, elbowing aside the Jack Daniels bottle. "I told you, no one's going to drink that fruity garbage...we aren't sorority girls, Abel."

"Speak for yourself." Abel crashes the seltzer cans down next to the pizza before carefully fixing the perfect cuffs of his mint-colored linen shirt. "I am a sorority girl now and forever."

"We didn't even *have* sororities at Prairie," Tracey reminds him. She pushes her short mane of curly hair behind her ears; Tracey and I share similarly loopy hair, although hers is dark walnut in color, and goes more for spirals while mine sticks to bouncy waves. And if I'm fairly short, Tracey is almost a miniature; she barely hits five feet and has a tendency to disappear in crowded subway cars. To avoid losing her on group outings, we usually keep her close to Abel, who is a towering six-foot-four.

"*I* was the sorority at Prairie Arts," Abel announces loftily. "The one and only." He cracks open a pineapple hard seltzer and tips it back.

We're still shaking our heads at him when a slim red-head in a pretty blue dress appears in the open doorway—Caitlyn, bearing a paper bag from the sushi place on First Avenue that advertises a California roll happy hour.

"Hey guys," she calls. "Can I come in?"

Caitlyn *always* asks before coming in. Like me, she was an outsider who joined this little college trio after they got to New York, but she remains somewhat distant despite our entreaties that she just act like one of the gang.

"Would you come in already?" Margot demands, throwing up her hands. "Stop acting so polite and be a rowdy member of this household like we have asked."

"You don't ever have to ask to come in," Abel tells her, crumpling his seltzer can in one giant hand. "I would never expect that of you."

"*You* don't live here," Tracey reminds him. "But Caitlyn, honey, it's true."

Caitlyn smiles uncertainly, as if she hasn't heard this at least three dozen Saturdays in a row. "Thanks. I'll try to remember."

"You always say that." Margot looks at her phone. "Oh, good news! Dane is coming."

I draw in a single, harsh breath, but no one hears me.

Tracey drops the lid of the pizza box she's been peering into. "You're joking! We haven't seen him in forever! I didn't even know he'd moved to the city."

"I know. But we ran into him at the cafe this morning, right, Maeve?"

I'm trying to pull myself together, but my heart's racing and my hands are shaking. My stomach doesn't feel so great, either. Like someone tipped a bag of cotton balls down my throat and they're all glomming together into one mass in my middle.

Dane is coming *here?*

So he really does know everyone?

How can I not remember this?

"Maeve?" Margot tips her head curiously. "Remember how you saw Dane this morning at the cafe?"

"R-right," I stammer. "We met him there."

Margot gives me a funny sort of smile.

Get it together, Maeve!

"Well, that's exciting," Tracey declares. "Good thing I got so much pizza. He won't mind if we start now, right? I'm starving."

And she starts flinging paper plates at us like Frisbees.

While everyone else starts tucking in, I excuse myself to go to the bathroom and clean up. I need a minute alone to absorb all this.

Their tiny bathroom is tiled in white, with a narrow window overlooking an alley four floors below. The window is open, allowing the evening breeze to filter in, along with street noise and a few dry leaves from the locust tree growing near the stoop. I can hear a bus lumbering along the avenue a half-block away. I listen to the air escaping its brakes and think, Dane might be getting off that bus right now.

And then what happens? He comes up here and I somehow give myself away?

Maybe this is for the best, I tell myself. Maybe they'll reminisce about how we all met, and it'll be out in the open.

Or maybe someone will ask me about our first meeting, and I'll have to run out of the apartment and never come back. I'll have to pretend work is calling and I'm needed in Central Park right away. Landscaping emergency. Flowers in peril.

Yeah, that'll convince them.

I feel flushed and sweaty. This whole thing is just too stressful. There's a *reason* I don't date anymore. There's a *reason* I haven't told my friends about my memory condition. I can't keep relationships going when people know about it, and I can't keep the charade going when they don't.

But here I am, trying to do it all again.

I run cold water in the sink and splash my neck and chest, wishing I could just dunk my whole head under the tap. If it had just been the usual gang out there, I might have gone for it. But with Dane coming over? I have a stupid, misguided need to look my best for this guy.

This guy who acts like he knows me. This guy I can't remember for the life of me.

This guy who already spent the whole damn morning trying to charm me, and succeeded.

Chapter Six

I HEAR THE front door open and the choruses of "Dane!" before I make it out of the bathroom.

Great, now I'm coming out of the room with the toilet. What a stunning entrance. I open the door as quietly as I can, but there's nowhere to hide in a tiny apartment like this. So I step into the living room with a sheepish expression, wishing my hot cheeks would just cool down already.

Dane is standing by the kitchen island, looking impossibly gorgeous. He's cleaned up since this morning's walk in the park, wearing a brown-and-white check shirt and a pair of slim jeans. His hair falls softly over his forehead, and I want to reach up, push it back into place, look into his hazel eyes with those little glistening chips of gold, and kiss his full lips until we melt together.

Oh, Maeve. Why do this to yourself? I hesitate, hand on the back of the bathroom door, as if I might head right back in before he sees me.

And then it's too late. Dane looks across the room at me, and his face lights up. In fact, he looks so pleased to see me, it's like he's read my mind and knows I was just thinking about kissing him.

My brain goes absolutely wild at his expression. He likes me! He spent all morning with me, and now, a bare six hours later, he's ready to spend more time with me!

And I feel the same way about him!

Okay, heart, slow down, I tell my hammering pulse. *Don't be so obvious.*

As if Dane can look into my chest and see my crazy heart slamming away in there, overwhelmed with pleasure at seeing him again.

"Hey, Maeve," he says gently.

"Hey, Dane," I reply, impressed with my lips for forming actual words.

Tracey, standing next to Dane, looks slowly from my face to Dane's, then back to me. Her eyes widen ever so slightly.

Abel is opening another hard seltzer and doesn't notice that conversation has suddenly screeched to a halt.

But Margot does. "How great is it having Dane back?" she asks the room at large. "I thought we'd never see this guy again."

"Great," Tracey agrees, giving me a significant smile.

My heart skips a beat, then starts pounding again. This time, though, it's for all the wrong reasons. I can't deal with knowing glances and secret smiles. Not when I don't know what any of it's about.

I want to talk to Dane for the rest of the night, but not here. I want to drag him out the front door, down the creaky staircase, out onto the stoop, maybe right down the block. Away from my friends and the nostalgic conversation that's sure to give me away and ruin everything.

Oh, god. This is Angela Krebs all over again.

Maybe I've been making a mistake, living my whole life with this secret about my faulty memory from the world. But so far, nothing has happened to prove me wrong. I've had guys ditch me, I've had girls stop inviting me places. And it all started with Angela Krebs, my best friend in the fifth grade.

Angela was the one who taught me, just a few months after a station wagon knocked me off my bike and headfirst into a curb, that my memory loss would always be a secret shame. Something to be hidden—at least, if you wanted to keep your friends.

It was just an invitation to sleep over. Not anything major, not a birthday or anything like that. But when Angela's mother called mine, demanding to know why I'd promised to come over to stay the night and then hadn't shown up, just left Angela sitting by the door waiting, *crying* that her best friend in the world hadn't bothered to come like she'd said—well, then it turned into a much bigger deal than a missed summer sleepover.

My parents hadn't known that I'd been forgetting things at an abnormal rate. I was just a kid, so little clues like constantly blanking on homework assignments I hadn't written down were easily missed. Kids didn't pay attention. They zoned out in class. Stuff got missed. Normal, right?

Not normal, my doctor said. But there was nothing to be done. It was a lingering consequence of the concussion, and I'd have to learn to live with it.

The notebooks came soon after, an effective solution to accessing my locked memories, but Angela Krebs had already made her choice. Her new best friend was Shelby Langston, and I grudgingly admitted to myself that she was a good upgrade. Shelby's family had a pool.

Over the years, I told a few people about my condition, waiting until it seemed like we'd reached a good moment, a point in our relationship where the other person could accept I wasn't always going to remember our plans, and that I'd be writing down notes on everything we did and said together. That, overall, I was a broken version of a person. It rarely worked out.

Those sharing moments became fewer and farther between, and until my high school friend Todd moved to the city a few months ago, no one in New York City knew about my memory disorder.

That was on purpose. By the time I got to New York, I'd learned my lesson about opening my mouth to people who aren't as invested in me as I am in them. I've learned a lot of lessons over the years.

I keep copious notes to avoid accidentally ruining another friendship. I don't tell my rare dates about my situation. And I keep what goes into my notebooks secret. Margot is convinced it's bad poetry. Tracey thinks I'm working on some creative nonfiction project. Abel is so busy being Abel, he doesn't have time to think about what I might be doing. Caitlyn keeps her thoughts to herself. And I don't take notes in front of my coworkers.

It's my secret.

It's going to stay that way.

I've gotten along this far without telling them; why should anyone need to know now?

"Maeve," Tracey says, "can I get you another drink?"

"Many drinks," I reply, finding my empty cup and brandishing it. "Pizza Saturday, everyone!"

"Pizza Saturday!" my friends roar, the silence forgotten as we launch into our favorite toast. Dane joins in, holding up his cup, and I'm struck by how easily he fits in, like he's always been part of Pizza Saturday and our little circle of friends. Like he's been here forever.

I feel disoriented, but honestly, at this point in my life that's nothing new.

Chapter Seven

"So, THEY BASICALLY acted like old friends all evening." I shake my head. "It was confusing, Todd."

My old high school buddy Todd pokes his finger into his cold brew and shoves an ice cube around. "Does this look like a bug to you? Or is it coffee grounds? Maybe it's just coffee grounds."

"You've probably consumed both of those things already today," I say impatiently. "Can you focus on my problem, please?"

He leans back in his chair and obediently faces me. Todd has a mobile, rubbery face, perfect for his job as an improv actor. He uses it now to shove his expression into one of grave concern, like he just found out a deadly spy is in our midst. "You know, someone could use that against you," he says.

"What? Use what against me?"

"Your memory issues."

"They don't know about them."

"Come on, Maeve. I figured it out in about ten seconds."

"Because your father is a neurologist!"

"Well, *I'm* not a neurologist. As my family loves to remind me at each and every holiday gathering."

"No, but you would have absorbed some of it. Dinner-table conversation, that kind of thing. But okay. Let's say he knows about my memory issues. How could he use that against me?"

Todd shrugs noncommittally, like he hasn't thought this through. Big surprise. Todd spends ninety-nine percent of every conversation thinking about his own life. He says, "It's just that everything is such a scam now. When's the last time you answered your phone? *Exactly,*" he continues as I make a grossed-out face. "Maybe I'm crazy, but I think everything is a scam these days. And it seems to me like someone could fake knowing you, embarrass you into going with it, then abuse your trust to get money out of you. Or something like that. Or they could do an identity theft, however that works. Don't you ever think about things like this?"

"Well, I didn't before!" Todd's worldview is seriously depressing. Having a comedic actor for a friend should be more fun.

"You can't trust anyone. That's what I'm getting at. Not even me," Todd adds dramatically.

"Oh, shut up. I've known you since you were snorting milk out your nose to get laughs."

"It still works," he says, prodding again at the mystery speck in his iced coffee. "You have no idea, the audiences we get in that stupid club. Total bumpkins. One guy last week wanted to know why our show didn't have any *juggling.*"

"Maybe you should move on from the free comedy place just outside Times Square? Just a thought."

"Sure, I'll go work at The Late Show as soon as they call me back." Todd pushes the coffee away, looking disgusted. "I've only sent them fourteen resumes over the past five years."

"I don't know. I just feel like you'd have a better shot at getting discovered if you were working some edgier clubs. Maybe in Brooklyn, or..."

"Comedy, in Brooklyn?" Todd snorts. "You know nothing about this business. And Brooklyn is *not* the funny borough."

I don't have the energy to pursue that one. I'm still chewing over his scam idea. "Do you really think he's faking it? But what about everyone else? My other friends? They'd have to be in on it."

"Yeah, that's true. Of course, how well do you really know them?"

"I've known them almost a year!" He is *not* taking Margot, Tracey, Caitlyn, and Abel from me. I *need* them. They're a lifeline in this city. Todd may be an old friend, but he's hardly ever free to hang out. Too busy pursuing fame and fortune to do things like commit to Saturday night pizza dates, and out too late on weeknights to hang out with me. Maybe my early-morning job has made me old before my time, but I'm usually in bed asleep before Todd gets off work and hits his first bar of the night.

"How well do we know anyone?" Todd goes on, and I suspect he isn't even talking to me anymore. He's just fumbling around with some philosophical nonsense. When Todd isn't writing comedy or fooling around onstage for tourists, he's writing long-winded essays for literary magazines with strange titles like *Ghoul Economy* or *Communist Cat Fanciers Club*. It is truly an unholy blend of interests. "Everyone is keeping their own secrets, as a defense against a world they're afraid won't want them."

"Please stop," I beg. "Or I will leave."

"You should go anyway," Todd says cheerfully. "I have to go. I have a show in twenty."

I stare at him before protesting, "But I thought we were having Fake Date Night later! At the fancy place on West Fiftieth! Look, I'm already wearing my new sparkly shoes." I extend one leg from under the table so he can see my rhinestone-studded Converse. "I had to break them in before I pair them with a swanky cocktail dress later."

"Check your notebook again," Todd advises me with a smirk. "Because I told you last week that I was taking this show for Jonathan. He had to go back to Michigan to deal with his sick uncle or something."

Another notebook fail? This is getting systemic. I rub at my eyes; luckily I haven't put on my Fake Date Night makeup yet. "I can't believe I missed that. I was all excited about fancy appetizers. And I was going to make you split a tiramisu with me. Are you *sure* you canceled on me?"

Todd folds his rubber face into serious lines and throws me a dead-eyed stare. Tonelessly, he drones, "Or maybe I'm gaslighting you and this is all a scam. What's real and what's fake, Maeve Benson?"

"Todd! Stop it!"

He laughs. "I'm sorry, couldn't resist. Okay, I'm taking you to the fancy romance restaurant on West Fiftieth next—" he makes a show of checking his phone's calendar before deciding, "Next Tuesday. I'll make a reservation. Most romantic table."

"You better dress sexy," I remind him. "We used to dress sexy for Fake Date Night. Let's bring back the old traditions."

"I always dress sexy." Todd plucks at the collar of his button-up shirt, which is patterned with tiny fish. "Oh, this old thing? Dead sexy."

"Wear a tie," I demand. "I'm going to wear a little black dress."

"And those shoes, I hope."

"Of course, these shoes. That's why I *bought* them."

Todd heads off to his club, leaving me with the dregs of my latte and a sour feeling about life in general. I'd been genuinely excited for Fake Date Night, something we'd come up with back when he was doing comedy in Albuquerque and I was just a country vocational school mouse, coming to shows to cheer him on. People thought we were dating, which we most emphatically were not, but Todd couldn't resist a good bit. So we embraced their whispers by enjoying the most indulgent date nights possible on our tight student budgets. Fake Date Night became my favorite part of every month, and I missed it when I moved to New York the summer after graduation.

So, when Todd got to New York six months ago, we made it a point to bring back our monthly Fake Date Night, although the dress code had slipped of late.

Well, now I need new dinner plans. I flip through Yelp on my phone, looking for anything new to the neighborhood in my price range. Slim pickings. My friends are always telling me the Upper West Side was probably not the best part of the city for a girl in her mid-twenties, and they're absolutely right. I'd just happened to luck into an apartment from a coworker moving out of state soon after I'd started at the park, and it seemed crazy not to accept a rent-controlled studio so close to my job that I didn't even need a rainy-day bus route.

And there is the Cafe & Croissant factor, too. Living near a really good cafe is a good reason to hang onto an apartment, even if the neighborhood isn't perfect for me. The baristas are kind and fun. The cafe opens early enough for me to stop in on the way to work. And of course, that's where I met Dane.

For the second time, according to him and everyone.

Everyone but me.

So far, I've seen Dane twice since Saturday night. On Sunday, we bumped into each other at the market at Eighty-first and Amsterdam. He was buying avocados and French bread; I was buying avocados and sourdough bread. We looked at each other's baskets in surprise and laughed together. "Hot night," I'd explained. "Salad days."

"My apartment gets to about a hundred and seventy degrees if I even use the toaster," Dane replied, grinning. "And that's with the AC running. Bashful makes me keep the place cool."

"Oh, you have an air conditioner? Lucky!"

"I know, it's the dream." His smile gave me warm tingles all over. There was no other way to describe it.

Of course, it was really hot in the market.

Wasn't it? It sure seemed that way.

Anyway, we just kind of gazed at each other until a determined senior citizen rammed both of us with her cart, and we found ourselves shoved in separate directions. Dane waved goodbye from the checkout, and I bought a pint of gelato to give myself a few extra minutes before I went onto the sidewalk after him. I thought he might have hung around to walk with me, but he was lost to the crowds on Amsterdam Avenue.

Then yesterday afternoon, just an average weekday after work, I saw him walking home from the subway. Crisp white shirt, slim navy pants, shiny brown oxfords—he'd clearly been at work. He'd told me he had a boring office job, and I believed him, but there was nothing wrong with his office style.

I'd been picking up a bottle of wine at a shop on Broadway when his brisk stride caught my attention. He might have been anyone, but my eyes found him instantly, and they followed him as he strolled confidently down the block and turned up Eighty-fifth Street. It was a huge effort not to chase after him, but I managed. He hadn't sent me a text or anything since our double-trouble Saturday. A Saturday night in which everyone had managed to talk about everything except when we'd all met Dane. My fears of getting caught forgetting didn't come true, but it's going to come up, eventually. It has to. And what's going to happen then?

I'd rather not think about it.

But either way, I haven't talked to him since we met in the market. Which means it's possible I won't see him again until Saturday night rolls around again...and this time, it'll be just as friends. He clearly doesn't want to date me.

This is for the best. I can't get involved with him romantically, not when he's in the group. Because it won't work out, and then things will get awkward. And yes, I know for a fact it won't work out.

It hasn't worked out with *anyone* so far; my track record with dating was dismal, to say the least. Since I moved to New York, I've practically been a nun; my Fake Date Nights with Todd are the most action I've seen in months.

Even if it wasn't so hard to meet people here—everyone is in a hurry, no one wants to slow down for five minutes and just have a chat with a friendly-faced stranger or a new coworker—I still have to *remember* them. And it's hard work jotting down notes about a date quickly enough that our conversation is still fresh in my mind. I can't keep track of anyone in New York; they're all darting around like dragonflies while I'm waving my pen feebly in the air, begging them to give me five minutes.

And judging by Dane's surefooted stride last evening as I watched him roll confidently along Broadway, he's just like the rest of them. Already assimilated to the New York City pace of life, even if he's only been here for a few weeks. Some people are just born for the rat race, I suppose.

"Miss, can I clear this table?" A young woman pauses alongside me, tray in hand. I reluctantly get up and let her take the empty glasses. She glances back at the door, where new customers are looking around for a table. That's my cue to leave.

Where to now, Maeve?

I didn't find anything on Yelp that looked even moderately appealing, so I decide I'll just head up Columbus, towards Cafe & Croissant. One cafe conquered, and on to the next. I'll have a sandwich and soup or something, then turn in early. Sleep this whole thing off.

The cafe I'd met Todd in was down near Columbus Circle, so it's a long tramp back up to the West 80s. Usually a summer evening walk up Columbus is a nice diversion. People eating outside on the sidewalk, the sky turning pink and navy blue above the high-rises and apartment blocks. But tonight the streets seem unusually loud. The crowds seem even more harried than usual. And I'm looking at every tall man on the pavement, wondering where Dane might be tonight.

So, I'm relieved when I finally step into Cafe & Croissant and pull the door closed behind me, blocking out the worst of the city's racket and whole blocks of lesser men. I take a breath and let the barely-there breeze of the air conditioning unit above the doorway tease the bare skin on my shoulders.

And then I see him, standing at the counter. His back is to me, but I'd recognize those broad shoulders anywhere.

I reach behind me, fumbling for the brass doorknob. Not now, not when I'm sweaty from my long walk and feeling anxious in general—

Dane turns around and once again, I have that cotton-ball feeling combined with a strange sense of fate.

Chapter Eight

"HEY, MAEVE!" HE calls. Not in the baseball-coach voice, thank goodness, but a normal cafe volume. "Fancy seeing you here again!"

Tilda's behind the counter this evening. She brushes back her mop of Little Mermaid-red curls and tosses me a suggestive grin. "Yeah, fancy that," she drawls in her Australian accent. "I thought you only came in here for every brekkie of the week. Supper, too? Is your microwave broken, Maeve?"

I scowl at her, but inside I'm thankful she's taken the focus off my unexpected reunion with Dane. "Would you rather I go home and nuke a Lean Cuisine, Tilda? Because I can leave."

"No, no, get out—I have one piece of banana bread left with your name on anyway," she says good-naturedly. "You can start on that, and I'll see if I can find you some soup." She pushes through the swinging door into the tiny kitchen.

Leaving me alone with Dane.

I mean, yes, there are a couple other people in the cafe, but it seriously feels like we are alone in the room. In the city. In time and space.

He runs his fingers through his hair, and suddenly I want to do the same thing. To him, I mean. I want to touch those soft brown locks. I want to skim my fingertips down his tanned cheek, along the firm line of his jaw. I want to stand so close to him I can feel the heat of his body, and turn my chin up to look into his eyes, and—

"Banana bread, with honey and butter!" Tilda announces, bursting out of the kitchen. "No soup left, but I found an apple tart, so I'm throwing that in—"

Her gaze flicks between us. Then our eyes meet, and her grin grows so wide she could swallow me whole. "I'll get you two a second fork," she says.

I protest this intimacy, obviously, but Tilda is overpowering and soon we find ourselves in a table by the window while she bustles through closing up the kitchen and bakery counter. The other patrons take the hint—Tilda has a tendency to crash dishes together and can make more noise washing dishes than most people can handle—and soon enough, Dane and I are alone, picking through the banana bread and apple tart she gave us. With *two* forks, as promised.

One plate, though. Tilda's generosity does not extend to an extra dish she will have to wash. Or maybe she just wants to force us to share.

We work around each other's forks carefully, slicing up in the bread and tart in the most equitable way we can. Things feel almost stiff between us as the silverware clatters against the plate, and I wonder if that moment by the bake case had only been my imagination.

Or a mistake. Maybe everything we'd done on Saturday—the long walk with Bashful, the hot dogs for lunch, then the friendly gathering at Margot and Tracey's apartment—had been just that…friendly. Maybe there'd never been any intention here.

Maybe we're just friends.

That will be okay, of course. That'll be great! Everyone needs more friends. You can't have too many people to sit around cafes with! And Dane lives in the neighborhood, and I'm sure to see him in passing all the time. Just great. Just super.

Just fantastic.

The apple tart and banana bread taste of nothing to me now, but I plow through them, anyway. I'm tough. I can handle this. And it isn't really rejection if we're still friends, right?

Dane pushes the last piece of apple tart my way. "I haven't had this much butter in a year," he says. "You finish it, I'm dying here."

"Maybe you can do a few extra reps at the gym," I joke, spearing the piece of pastry with my fork. He's fit enough, but

Dane doesn't look like a gym bunny to me. Plus, those guys usually loudly announce their gym routines. Repeatedly.

Dane grins and glances pointedly at his arms. "So you noticed the twins!"

I can't quite stifle my snicker at that, and his grin grows wider.

"These are real babe magnets, you know," he goes on, pretending to flex. Or maybe *pretending* isn't the right word. Dane obviously isn't a bodybuilder, unless he just started yesterday, but he isn't a string bean, either. "I can't wear a sleeveless shirt, because it's not fair to the ladies. I cause a stampede wherever I go. Gotta keep them covered up." He looks around to make sure we're really alone, then raises one humped bicep and gives it a smacking kiss.

I hear a snicker from behind the counter. "Tilda saw that," I inform him. "Now you can never come here again."

"Three strikes rule!" Tilda calls. "That's one, muscle man!"

Dane tugs down his sleeves. "Can't risk any more," he tells me. "Where else would I sit and wait for you?"

I look down at our cups. Now he's just confusing me.

I realize that I need to know what we're doing here. Not knowing what our future might be feels even more confusing than not knowing where we began.

Maybe you should just tell him.

The thought comes out of nowhere, like an express train racing past on a local track. Unexpected, unwelcome, and with the potential to sweep me right off the platform. I cling to the safety of solid ground, reminding myself there's a million reasons why I keep my memory a secret. Obviously, I can't tell him. I *like* this guy.

I failed at dating a dozen times back in school because I was foolish enough to tell the truth, and this is New York—the competition in the dating pool is ten times as intense as it was back in my hometown. Right now, within a ten-block radius, there are a thousand single girls under age twenty-nine, all of them hotter and more successful and unencumbered by weird memory issues, waiting to pounce on the next handsome and successful man to walk past their hiding place.

A girl like me doesn't stand a chance against those wandering wolf-packs of beautiful women, and yet here I have a handsome, successful, nice man interested in me.

Am I really going to risk whatever shot I have with this him by giving away my awful truth?

No, the thing to do right now is figure out if Dane is really interested in dating me, or if he's simply joined my group of friends.

Let that express train race on by without me; I am sticking to the slow and steady local.

Tonight, I just need to know if this is merely a friendly cup of coffee and dessert, or a shared meal weighted with intention.

Tilda finishes crashing her crockery in the sink and pulls the cash out of the register, taking it into the kitchen to count and put away in the safe. Without the banging and splashing, I realize we're being very quiet.

And now we're alone.

"The thing is, I live near here," Dane says, breaking the silence. "On Eighty-fifth. That's why I was here tonight, I mean. I walked Bashful and then I felt like I wanted a cup of coffee. I wasn't *stalking* you or anything."

I blink, embarrassed at the way I'd watched him walk down the street. Who's the weird stalker now?

Dane coughs to smother a laugh. "Sorry, was that a bad word choice?"

"Not your best," I say, but I can't help smiling. The mood feels lighter. I touch my face, my neck, feeling foolish, then blurt, "Maybe you should tell me about your biceps again. Do you have triceps to match?"

Dane leans forward. The gold flecks in his eyes seem to smolder and spark under the cafe's warm lighting, and I feel my breath catch in my throat. He opens his lips to say something suggestive, I just know it. I place my fingers on my thighs, waiting anxiously. "Let me tell you something about my triceps," he purrs. "I know the ladies love them, I know they drive them wild, but, Maeve?"

The way his tone caresses my name! My skin is sizzling with anticipation.

Dane draws a breath, then delivers the final blow. "I have *no* idea where those things are."

The hysterical laughter I burst into is probably more about my humming, live-wire nerves than how funny his joke is, but Dane looks pretty pleased, anyway. He surveys our empty cups and plate, then pulls out his wallet and places a ten on the table. A generous tipper. Is there anything *not* to like about this guy?

"We seem to be finished here," he says. "And Tilda wants to lock up. Let me walk you home."

Oh, my!

Chapter Nine

I LIVE ON the second floor of an old brownstone on Eighty-first Street, a back apartment overlooking a neat little terrace kept in perfect order by the first floor family. On summer nights, this family tends to spill onto their terrace and stay out there until nine or ten at night, and my apartment can get hazy with barbecue smoke, loud with kids shouting and playing. Not exactly setting the mood I'm hoping for.

Tonight, thank goodness, they've gone out. My apartment's open windows let in only the distant sounds of traffic on Amsterdam Avenue, filtered from a roar to a buzz by layers of trees and buildings, and the rustling leaves of the locust tree at the back of the yard.

I breathe a little sigh of relief, along with a silent thank you to whichever gods are in charge of romantic trysts. Because I am pretty sure we are moving firmly into that territory. Judging by the look in Dane's eyes as he follows me up the stairs, I am in for at *least* an intense make-out session on the sofa.

But first, I have to clear up my mess.

He stops in the doorway and takes in the state of my apartment with widened eyes. Instantly, I see myself demoted in his eyes, from potential kissing partner to possible sociopath.

And of course he can't know I tore the place apart because of *him.*

It had been Sunday, the first chance I'd gotten to go through my old journals and try to piece together when I'd met Dane. And despite hours of rummaging and reading, I hadn't found the answer. For some reason, I'd skipped writing on whatever day our meeting had been.

And so, until something finds its way through my brain to free that memory, it's lost to me.

Late Sunday night, aware I had work early in the morning, I'd given it up and gone to bed, leaving behind a pile of notebooks. But every evening since, I've tried again.

Long story short, the place is still a mess.

I watch Dane drag his gaze around the upturned books on the shelves, the pile of pillows next to the sofa, and the up-ended storage ottoman, and I *almost* blurt out, "I've been robbed!"

Thank goodness my brain gets control of my tongue halfway through the sentence, so what comes out is, "I've been—cat-sitting."

Brilliant work, Maeve. Everyone knows cats are terrors.

Dane glances at me, eyebrows raised. "Were you cat-sitting a tiger?"

"Just a regular old tabby-cat! Hahaha!"

Oh, now it's time for the nervous laughter that is a few decibels too high! Super!

I start picking up pillows and sowing them along the sofa like a farmer with her seeds as I continue my dumb cat story. "She was, um, really into playing? So the place got kind of torn up. She's gone now," I add quickly, as I see Dane's eyes sweep over the open window and widen with alarm. "Went home last night! Late. Too late for me to clean up before work. And I met a friend after work, and then I went to the cafe, and now here we are!"

I make myself stop before I sound any more hysterical.

"Got it. Well, let me help you." And before I can stop him, Dane picks up the topmost journal on the pile of notebooks balanced next to the ottoman. To my horror, he *opens* one. Why would he do that?

"These are pretty books," he begins, then he realizes what he's looking at. "Oh, gosh, this is a journal, isn't it? I'm so sorry." He snaps it shut and places it back on the pile, looking guilty. "I didn't realize they were journals. I wasn't prying into your secrets, honest."

God, he'd looked. What might he have seen? What year was that journal from? What if he'd opened it to a date? What if he'd opened it to a *bad* date, pretty much the only kind I ever went on, reduced to bullet points. One time I'd gone out with a guy and all I'd bothered to write down was:

- *gyro cart on Seventh*
- *squirrel attack*
- *emergency room*
- *no future here*

He's going to think I'm a sociopath.

(For the record, the squirrel attacked the guy, he only needed six stitches, and it seemed like a sign from my guardian angel.)

This is a disaster. My breath is coming so fast, I am pretty sure I'm about to hyperventilate. I look around for a paper bag, but dismiss the idea before I find anything to breathe into. It will be far less embarrassing to just faint dead away, rather than to start panting into a hat or something.

"They're—it's—nothing," I manage. "Don't worry about it, please. Let me just—" I start picking up the notebooks stacked on the sofa. There's still a chance at that make-out session.

Or at least a cuddle? We can work up to it.

Dane begins straightening up my messy bookshelves, as if he needs to be cleaning, too. Does he studiously keep his back to me as I scramble to get my notebooks shoved into my storage ottoman and safely out of sight? If so, I'm sure if I feel more grateful or embarrassed. I'll have to settle for a blend of both.

I slam the top onto the ottoman and push it against the wall next to the TV table. Then I give myself ten seconds to shake out my hair and put on a normal, non-crazy-person smile before

I say, "Hey, don't worry about those old books. I'll get it all fixed up later."

"Oh, I don't mind," Dane says, but he leaves the bottom shelf untidied, anyway. He smiles at me as he goes on, saying, "I like to get a measure of the person I'm with by checking out her books. This was just an excellent excuse for me to do a quick character assessment."

"A book-snob, huh? I like it. Tell me how you're grading my taste and then I'll tell you if you can stay in my apartment." I fold my arms across my chest, liking where this is going. I happen to have *excellent* taste in books.

"A lot of romance on this shelf," Dane begins, running his finger along a line of some of my most well-worn paperbacks. "Which means—"

"Absolutely nothing?" I interrupt. Of *course* he goes for the romances first. Men love picking on women for reading romance novels, as if their trashy thrillers with lots of explosions and sexy assassins are somehow Harvard-level reading.

"It means you like a happy ending," he continues. "Right?"

His smile seems to tug at something deep inside me. "Well," I allow, "we all like happy endings. Don't we?"

"Some people say they're not artistic," he says blandly, testing my resolve. "Some people say only sad endings are true art."

"Well, some people are idiots."

"And here," Dane goes on, grinning devilishly at me like I answered exactly the way he hoped, "we have some travel books. Some pretty exotic locales. Patagonia, really?"

I shrug. "I want to travel."

"Fair enough. But I'm really interested in these—" Dane runs a finger along the books I keep on the middle shelf, just below eye-level. "You have a *lot* of books about the brain and cognitive function, Maeve."

"Oh, well…" I don't know if I have a lot. Eight, tops. "The brain is interesting."

"I don't know anything about it, to be honest." He tugs out a paperback and thumbs through it. I hope it isn't one I've made notes in. A few of them are heavily highlighted and have penciled notes in the margins—remnants of my high school years, when I'd thought maybe I could research my way out of my memory problems. But they weren't exactly textbooks, and it turned out popular science didn't hold the keys to curing my brain. In the end, I'd stuck to my notebooks. I only hang onto the books because, well, who can throw out a book?

"This is heavy stuff," Dane says, putting the book back in its place. He looks at me. "You're a dark horse, Maeve."

I feel myself blushing and look at the floor. "I'm really not."

"No, seriously. Did you understand that book? It was a lot of gibberish to me."

"Honestly, it's not that complicated, but it helps if you read the whole thing. You can't just open it in the middle and hope for the best." I glance around my half-tidied apartment and feel all my past elation go up in frustrated smoke. The light outside my window is a luminous blue. Sunset has come and gone; it must be close to nine o'clock and we both have work in the morning and instead of locking lips, we are talking about my big freaking brain. Which isn't a genius brain at all, despite Dane's earnest implication that it is. This is a broken, irreparable, shattered brain.

I feel like screaming. I know Dane, but I don't know him. And he thinks he knows me, but he doesn't know me. And neither do my friends. No one knows me in this whole damn city. All people can do is look at me and make a guess, and they'll never come close to being right.

But if they knew the truth, they'd scatter. Because having a friend with a memory disorder is—well, it's *disorderly*. It's a pain in the ass. And people in this city don't think twice about ditching people who are a pain in the ass. There are plenty of people on the street with normal, ambitious, money-hungry, New York City brains. They don't need my broken one slowing them down.

"What's the matter?" Dane's voice softens; as twilight gathers around my dim studio, his strong features seem to glow. "You look sad."

"I'm not sad," I say, struggling to get hold of myself. *I'm not sad, I'm just disappointed that you came back here to kiss my face off and instead we're talking about my books and my mess and I'm realizing that you're never going to be into me.*

"Hey," Dane says, and suddenly he crosses the space between us, floorboards creaking beneath him, and puts his hand on my chin. "Listen, I'm sorry if I was picking on you about your books. I didn't mean it like that. I'm impressed by you, that's all."

"It's fine," I whisper, shaken to the core by the soft warmth of his fingertips on my skin. "I shouldn't be so sensitive."

"I like that you're sensitive," he tells me, lowering his voice to match mine. "I happen to be pretty sensitive, too."

And he dips his lips to mine and gives me the sweetest, most sensitive kiss of my life.

I walk Dane to the front door of my building and stand on the stoop to watch him go. He only lives a few blocks away, but I still hate to see him leave. If he hadn't knocked over a potted fern with an elbow while we were entwined on the sofa, he might not have gone so soon.

But the fern reminded him I was a gardener, and remembering I was a gardener reminded him that I had to be at work at seven in the morning, and then he got very concerned about what time my morning alarm went off and not keeping me up all night. Boom, successful make-out session gets a rain delay, despite my protests that I can do just fine on four hours of sleep.

"No, no, that's no good," Dane insisted, fixing the buttons on his shirt while I straightened my blouse and tried to keep a smile on my face.

Seems like Dane can be a little *too* thoughtful, is what I'm saying here.

He turns back at the corner near Amsterdam, just to wave goodnight. I lift a hand to wave back. We're still only about six stoops apart, close enough to yell to one another. I almost shout, "Just come back here!"

But before I can, someone else yells, "Make me a drink, Maeve. Date night is back on!"

I whirl around. Todd is coming from the opposite direction, looking extremely happy and very inebriated. He sees me looking his way and whoops. The sound echoes off the elderly brownstones lining our end of the street.

"Dude," I shout-hiss. "Quiet neighborhood hours! Shut *up!*"

"Oh, I forgot you lived in the old folks' home," Todd laughs. "Sorry, olds! Sorry, sorry!"

A window slams in the brownstone next door. Great. They'll be bitching about young renters at the next block association meeting. "Just *shhh,*" I tell him fiercely. "Stand on the stoop and behave while I wave goodnight—" I turn, anxious to finish the night right.

But Dane is already gone, his spot on the corner filled by a woman pushing a stroller and a man walking a pair of dachshunds.

My shoulders slump. I really wanted that last wave goodnight. Just so he goes home knowing I'll be thinking about him tonight.

"So, wait, were you talking to someone else?" Todd leans against the newel post and regards me with interest. "Maeve Benson, you sly wench! Was *that* The Guy?"

"It was," I admit. "I was waving goodnight to him when you screamed like a crazy person and woke up half the block. He probably thought you were the Riverside Park coyote and ran for his life." The coyote's been in the tabloids recently, and most New Yorkers are acting as if the sky is falling every time it's spotted.

"I don't believe there's really a coyote. That's someone's ugly dog. Anyway, shouldn't he have come back and saved you? What kind of man is he? *I* would have saved you." Todd flexes. It is not as impressive as when Dane did it. Or maybe I am biased. He goes on, "Anyway, I have amazing news. I've been discovered. My Times Square improv days are over!"

I stare at him, surprise shoving aside my disappointment. "You're kidding! What happened?"

"Sit down and I'll tell you everything. Or better yet, invite me up and give me a drink and I'll *still* tell you everything, but with a drink."

I look him over, considering his inebriation and its potential to destroy my few possessions. A sofa can only take so much. "A cup of tea," I counter. "You've had plenty to drink tonight."

"Done," Todd agrees, unconcerned, and I know he'll probably throw a dollop of whiskey in his tea, anyway. He slopes up the stairs with a fluid motion. "Up we go."

I cast one more glance over the empty sidewalk, feeling a pinch of disappointment. He's really gone home. But at least I'll see him again.

And I know this was the kind of night I'll remember without trouble—although I'll make some notes, just to be sure.

Chapter Ten

MARGOT IS BEHIND the counter at Cafe & Croissant, her white-blonde hair pulled back in a loose ponytail and her expression one of utter exhaustion. "Another all-nighter in the art factory," she moans, placing a carafe of fresh-brewed coffee on its stand. "Tell me again why I decided to work opening shifts at a cafe all summer? I should be going to bed right now. This mural project is kicking my ass."

"The cafe owner promised to help you finance your mural project," I remind her. "Remember that?"

"Oh, right." Margot busies herself with the espresso machine. "I'm making you a lavender latte this morning," she informs me. "Because you're a flower girl."

"That makes me sound like a small child in a wedding party," I protest. "At least call me a flower *woman*."

"Okay, flower woman," Margot agrees. "Looking forward to a fun day of playing in the dirt?"

"Always." I lean on the counter, suddenly eager to spill the beans to someone. "Guess what happened last night."

She dribbles steamed milk into espresso, half-heartedly forming a leaf pattern. "It's too early to guess. Just tell me."

"I saw Dane."

She lifts her eyebrows. "You *saw* him or you *saw* him."

"Umm...I *saw* him?"

Margot puts down the milk pitcher and squeals with delight. "You *saw* him? Oh my God! You little stinker!"

"I think I did! But I'm really not sure what we're talking about here! Maybe you could tell me!" I try really hard to match her energy, but once Margot is rolling, it's always hard to keep up.

"How far did things go?" Margot demands. The bell rings over the front door and her blue eyes shoot lasers at whatever hapless early-morning customer has just walked in. "A customer! Quick, tell me everything in ten seconds."

"We split pastries here and then we went to my place and then we made out," I blurt, all in one breath.

"You *made out?*" Margot cackles. "Oh, this is excellent. Like the best parts of high school, without all the classes and gross people."

The new customer stands behind me and clears her throat.

"I can tell you more later," I assure her. "Although there's not really more to tell. That's basically the whole story."

"This is fantastic," Margot tells me, finishing up my drink. "I told Tracey the first time we all met that you two were going to be a thing. She owes me twenty bucks. I am so excited right now."

"Wait, you—" I'm struggling with what part of Margot's statement to question first. The first time we all met—she and Tracey made a bet about us getting together? Fine, I guess, but... Tracey bet *against* us?

The bell chimes and three more people waltz in, all talking over each other in cross, early-morning New Yorker voices. Margot and I sigh in unison.

"The drink is on the house," she says, shooing me away with my latte. "And we talk later."

Apparently, though, Margot can't wait until evening. I still have another hour on my shift and am down on my knees in a flower-bed, digging away contentedly, when she appears at my shoulder, nearly frightening me to death. "Good lord," I gasp, pushing to my feet and brushing dirt from my heavy work trousers. "Sneak up on a girl much?"

"I brought you a cold brew," she announces, thrusting a sweating cup at me. "I figured you could use a mid afternoon caffeine hit."

"I could, actually." I take the cup and sip gratefully. "Hmm... cinnamon?"

"And brown sugar, but I'm not sure how much that really comes through. It's something I'm working on. Cold drinks are harder."

"I wish I could write it down, but my notebook is back in my locker." We're on a little plot just north of the Sheep Meadow, surrounded by green slopes and a few chunks of hard Manhattan schist. Hooves clip-clop on the nearby park drive as a carriage horse passes by Bethesda Terrace. My locker at the landscape workers' base is a solid fifteen-minute walk away. I don't tend to worry about forgetting too much on my work shifts. I spend them digging in the dirt, my face in the flowers, while the world passes me by.

"Don't worry about it," Margot says airily, waving a hand. "You'll remember later."

I hope so. It's a pretty good drink. "Is this the only reason you came by? If so, good enough, and thank you."

She side-eyes me. "Hah! I *told* you I want to know everything about Dane."

"Oh, right!" The morning conversation comes flooding back into my mind, and I realize that until this moment, I'd completely forgotten I'd told her about my night with Dane. The nice thing about it, though, is I won't forget again; that isn't how this whole memory problem works. Stuff doesn't vanish forever in the depths of my brain; once my memory is jogged, the experiences are stored properly, some place where I can access them. For some reason, the first time around, things just don't stick in the right place.

I think back to my evening with Dane. "Well, we met up randomly, like I said. And then—um—"

And then I blink as I hit a brick wall in my brain. We had banana bread, I remember that much. But then my memory skips straight to the moment in my apartment where he picked up my notebook. Traumatic moments have a way of sticking. Naturally.

But so do ecstatic moments. And the hour that passed after that moment? Well worth remembering.

"We went to my place," I say finally. "And we kissed."

Margot nods impatiently. "Go on."

"We kissed *a lot.*"

Margot's lips stretches into a smile that is half leer. "Oh, you did, did you? How much is a lot? Did your clothes come off?"

"Some of them," I admit, but now I'm smiling too.

"Not all of them?" Margot shrugs and glances over my shoulder, as if something in the distance is more interesting than my boring, not-naked night with Dane. "Shame about that."

"Well, it was a work night." I gesture at my flower-bed. "He was respectful about my early alarm. Possibly too respectful, yes, but..."

"Oh, you've got yourself a real grown-up, all right. I bet he has a 401(k). I bet he has a *primary doctor.*"

"Don't be ridiculous," I scoff. "No one has a primary doctor. Definitely not anyone under thirty."

"Imagine if he did, though." Margot looks dreamy. "What a catch! He'd probably own his own apartment, too."

"And he'd take vacations. Real ones, not flying home for a week over the summer."

Margot is warming to our game. "And sometimes, when it's one o'clock in the morning and the express trains are all running local, he just calls an Uber, just like that."

"Not even an Uber," I say, upping the ante to ridiculous levels. "He just hails a cab. He doesn't even wait."

"You should marry this guy," Margot decides. "He's perfect for you. He's perfect for *me*."

"Margot, we just made all that up."

"Dammit, you're right." She flicks at a fly on the bodice of her fruit-patterned dress. "These are fake watermelons, bug. Well, I don't know, Maeve. He seems pretty put together. Maybe one of those things is true. One is really all it would take. I've never dated a guy with any one of those qualifications. Or a girl, either."

"I'd like for it to be the vacations," I admit. "Preferably cruises of the Mediterranean. I'd love to go to the Greek isles."

"On a private yacht," Margot suggests, "which is owned by his uncle, the childless Italian count."

"Who will leave him all his money? And his Venetian palazzo?"

"Okay, it's time to tie that down," she advises.

"The fake guy we're constructing, or Dane? I keep getting them mixed up."

"Oh, *either* of them," she sighs, gazing across the park towards the glittering heights of Midtown. "He's nice. That's more rare than a rich guy with a job, right? Just a really *nice* guy?"

She's so right about that.

I finish up the last half-hour of my shift while Margot heads back downtown to get some painting done. Or take a nap and then paint all night. Tracey always says it's usually the latter. She frequently comes home late from the gallery where she works as an assistant, passing out glasses of white wine and answering the phone, to find Margot making coffee and prepping for an all-nighter in the corner of the living room she calls The Art Factory. Luckily, Tracey is a heavy sleeper. Living with Margot would drive me crazy.

I don't mind working alone for the rest of the afternoon, or walking home along the shady park paths by myself. The park is alive with laughing children, chattering tourists, barking dogs, and chirping birds. Sometimes, Central Park is so loud with the sounds of life and fun, I can't even tell I'm still in the city. The illusion never lasts too long; every five or ten minutes, a siren wails from somewhere on the asphalt grid outside the park walls. But I savor every one of those moments when the city disappears—not because I don't want to be in New York City, but because I'm always thrilled with the power of the park to create its own happy, verdant bubble.

So I should be happy enough with my long solo walk back to the landscaping base, and the prospect of a stroll through the park on a bright, perfect afternoon like this.

Instead, I feel like I'm missing something.

I clock out, say goodbye to the supervisor, take my things from my locker, and start on my walk up to the Eighty-sixth Street park entrance, still feeling oddly discontented. My own company, and the park surrounding me, just aren't enough this afternoon.

And I think I know why. Oh, I've been spoiled by good company, and now I don't know how to do without it.

I'm hooked on Dane, alright. And when am I going to see him again? We didn't make any new plans. Why aren't we texting each other and making dates and doing this thing right? Are we just assuming we'll continue to bump into one another in the little village of Manhattan?

Because if so, that is a terrible plan. It's fine for things to fall to chance when you're just running into casual friends. But when something feels like it could be the real deal, you don't leave that up to the universe. You make it happen yourself.

I don't have to wait for him to text me, I decide. And I'm not going to wait for fate to bring us together one more time. Luck has never been my strong suit; I don't think the gods were particularly fond of me. Not out to get me, necessarily, but I'm not their favorite, either.

So I'm going to have to take matters into my own hands. When I get home, I'm going to send him a text. A text is not needy. A text is not stalker-ish. A text is just checking in, nailing down some dinner plans. It's all good.

Still, when I turn down Amsterdam Avenue, I don't mean to walk right past my turn at Eighty-first Street. I do notice when my feet don't round the corner, of course. I can still correct my route. I can pretend I was just going to over to the flower shop on the corner to buy myself something pretty to brighten up the apartment. Then, I'll turn right back around and head down my own street.

But I don't stop to buy a bouquet. I keep on walking, sauntering past the flower shop.

Maybe I'm just going to the produce market to get some fixings for a nice summer salad. It'll be too warm to cook in my little apartment tonight.

But I stroll on past the 82nd Street Grocery without even pausing to stroke Angelica Huston, the beautiful black cat who sits on the front stoop, watching the world go by, almost all day, every day.

Maybe I'm going to stop at...oh, forget it, Maeve! You aren't going to stop at any of those places. You are going to wander up and down Eighty-fifth Street and pretend you know where Dane lives. You are going to glance casually at some of the names on buzzers, to see if his last name pops out at you. You are going to hope that somehow, bizarrely, he'll get off work early and he'll come walking down the street, but of course there is *no* chance of that, you crazy—

I stop berating myself.

Because there he is, briskly stepping around the opposite corner, swinging onto Eighty-fifth from the direction of Broadway. He's wearing a suit—well, half a suit, he has the jacket flung over one arm—and a crisp white shirt with the sleeves rolled up, showing off his tan. A brown satchel hangs casually from one shoulder, bouncing along his hip as he walks with that swift, no-nonsense New York pace we only abandon in the park.

Dane is home from work early, and now what am I supposed to do?

Go and talk to him.

My inner voice is clearly crazy. I am sweaty and dirty from a day spent gardening. And I don't live on his street. It's a residential block, with no stores. So, he'll know I was just hanging around because I'm obsessed with him.

He'll love it.

No, he won't. He'll be freaked out.

He loves this kind of thing. It's so New York, people meeting up on the block. I want this for myself, someday.

I stop walking and stand on the corner, my hand on a newspaper box to steady myself. Was that—a memory? A ghost of a memory, anyway, a tiny, tantalizing link back to wherever, however, Dane and I first met. I wait, squeezing my eyes shut, begging the memory to materialize. But it doesn't, and when I open my eyes again, Dane is gone.

Chapter Eleven

I CAN'T GET up the nerve to text him after all. The near-meeting on his block, and the whisper of a memory as I watched him walking up the street, leaves me on edge all evening. I don't like knowing that there's a whole memory of him locked away, and it takes me until the next evening to shake off the discomfort.

It's too hot to cook dinner in my apartment, so late in the evening, I head back to Cafe & Croissant—*after* I've taken a very thorough shower, blow-dried my curls to a sleek wave, and put on a carefully chosen sundress in a summery pattern of turquoise and yellow.

New plan: I'll sit around and wait for him to show up, like it's a sign.

I *need* it to be a sign, like spotting him on the street must be a sign.

I need fate to bring us together, because I don't think I'm brave enough to do it. Not after the stalker-move on Eighty-fifth Street. I still can't believe I was lurking on his block, and then I just froze there, with my eyes closed, while he hustled to his building. He must have seen me.

God, I hope he didn't see me.

On the way to the cafe, I glance down at my feet in their cute turquoise slides and decide my toes could be better looking, so I pause at a salon on Amsterdam and get a pedicure. I emerge afterwards regretting every minute I just wasted in that chemical-scented storefront, but at least my toenails are a very feminine shade of pink, and my feet are so soft and smooth I kind of want to sit down and stroke them admiringly.

But that sort of thing isn't appreciated in public, so I scoot them under my table at Cafe & Croissant while ignoring curious stares from Mario, tonight's closing barista. He knows I'm not an evening regular, and he also knows I rarely wear dresses without cause.

It's possible the baristas here know *too* much about me. I'm starting to feel judged in my own hang-out.

Inspired by my turquoise outfit, Mario crafts me an iced Americano with a lingering aftertaste of coconut and vanilla. It makes me think of tropical islands, and I revise my dream of rich Dane's annual vacation. Now it will be a yachting cruise around the Caribbean, rather than the Mediterranean. Shorter flight to get there, anyway. We can go for Christmas.

Mario smiles when I take out my notebook and scribble down notes on his drink. He leans over the counter and pretends to squint across the room at the page. "You can name it, if you want," he offers. "I just came up with it for this warm day. I could put it on the menu tomorrow, but it needs a name. Got anything for me?"

I smile back at him and shook my head. I usually love naming drinks, but my head is definitely not in the game tonight. "Thanks, Mario. I'll think about it, okay?"

He gives me a little nod and goes back to his actual work, which is drawing a graphic novel in between helping customers.

I sit back in my chair and gaze through the front windows, trying to make Dane materialize. Or at the very least, grasp some shred of memory about the day we met.

But there's nothing on either front. Just the good people of the Upper West Side, scuttling home from work and after-school programs and sports.

I sigh over my Americano. It gets so frustrating sometimes. Even when I think I'm used to it, even when I believed I was doing great with my memory condition, there are still days when I can't quite get past how much it *sucks*. Just plain and simple sucks. I don't want to be a freak who can't remember the simplest things about my life without reading about it in a notebook. And I don't want to live a secret life that will never let me get truly close to other people. But this is what I got. The life I drew in the big old universal lottery.

And it sucks.

A single, self-pitying tear wells up in my left eye. Then one in my right. They hang there, balanced just above my eyelashes, ready to drop onto the blonde wood of the tabletop.

Then, a shadow falls over the table.

I look up.

He's here.

Once again, I've conjured him up. That has to mean something. This *has* to be something.

This can never be anything, because I can never tell him the truth.

I shove the thought away and smile up at him, brushing away the tears with a self-conscious little sniffle. "Dane! What are you doing here?"

"The same thing you're doing, I hope," Dane says softly. He takes the seat across from me and rests his hands on the table. I want to reach out and grab them, to squeeze those strong hands in my grip and feel how very warm and real he is. Not a pretty face I made up, not a mystery about my past I can't solve. Just Dane, a nice guy.

I remember Margot's words in the park. *He's nice. That's more rare than a rich guy with a job, right? Just a really* nice *guy?*

Dane might understand, I tell myself. He might get it. He might not think you're a freak.

"I was just having a little break from my apartment," I lie, instead of spilling my guts. "It's hot up there tonight."

"Writing a little poetry?" Dane nods at my notebook. "Margot told me that was your cafe thing. I could leave you alone if you want—"

"No, stay, I—"

My voice catches, but my mouth is still open, almost ready to tell him what's really in my notebook. But just then, Dane's gaze strays, his eyes following a pedestrian walking past the plate-glass window. And though I don't think he was doing anything out of order, just glancing up with natural interest as a person passes by, it's enough to stop me from confessing my problem. The stranger on the sidewalk is beautiful—no, the stranger on the sidewalk is smoking hot. She's one of those Manhattan women who somehow make their way around the city in stilettos and tight jeans and halter tops, like they aren't playing by the same rules as the rest of us. Her sleek hair ripples over her shoulders, and I have to stop myself from pressing a restraining hand over my own hair, which is already frizzing in the summer humidity.

She's what I'm up against.

I can't afford to be a freak in this city. I can't reveal myself as flawed in this metropolis stuffed to the gills with gorgeous women. I can't give up an inch of the ground I've clawed out for myself.

I'm not going to let this nice guy get up and leave me for something undamaged. Not when the odds are already so against my having caught his interest at all.

"The poetry's going great," I say, forcing a smile. It will feel real in a minute or two.

I've done it enough times to know.

Chapter Twelve

AND I'M RIGHT about it, too. Fake it until you make it? Honey, please. I am the queen of faking it. There should be Faking It Halls of Fame with me as the main attraction. You don't make it in New York City without a substantial amount of faking anyway, but when you don't remember a single face you pass on the street without a little help from your journal, life is all about pretending.

So I pretend. Because Dane has me enchanted, and I can't let him go.

For the rest of the long, steamy days of June, I smile and it is *real*. All of it. I smile so much my face hurts; I laugh until I cry; I kiss Dane until my lips feel swollen and full.

We go all over the city, and I remember at least half of every day. That's something—that means that every day we spend together is so magical and special, even *my* lumpy old mess of a brain can recall it without help. A miracle?

No, I think. Just Dane.

We walk his dog in the park and he points out the places where he coaches softball. I point out the gardens I've put in and the ones I'm still dreaming of taking over.

Dane thinks it's pretty funny that I call nearly everyone in the park 'tourists', so he decides we should put ourselves in their shoes and do some touristing of our own. We put together a wish-list, and together we visit Rockaway Beach, Flushing Meadows Park, The Cloisters—all the hot spots that are perfect for summers in the sunshine. And we seek out a few hidden gems, too, like the Little Red Lighthouse and City Island.

Everywhere we go, magic seems to follow. At a Cyclones game in Coney Island, we're spotted by the kiss cam and have to smooch to the chanting of *"Kiss, kiss, kiss"* from a thousand other fans. After the game, the Cyclone mascot himself takes our picture on the field, and Dane pronounces one of his lifetime goals complete.

"Your lifetime goal was to meet a giant seagull?" I ask skeptically.

"Surprisingly, yes," he laughs, pulling me close for one more kiss as they close the gates behind us. "A giant seagull at a baseball stadium along the Atlantic Ocean, as—" he pauses as a group of raucous teens goes past, jeering at us to just do it already, "—as our nation's youth applauds my achievement."

"Impressive achievements in kissing," I tell him, my lips at his neck, and we proceed to make out until a cop tells us to take it to the boardwalk with the rest of the deviants.

We get fried clam strips and shrimp from Ruby's and find a bench facing the ocean. It isn't a pretty evening by any estimation—the sea is steel-gray, the sky an indeterminate shade between brown and pink, and the western sky behind us has clouded over. The humidity suggests we'll have storms overnight. But I know I can't have wished for a more romantic evening if we'd gone off to Aruba or Hawaii or Key West. There is a charm to Coney Island that is indescribable: somehow, amidst the clatter of the roller coasters, the chiming of the arcade games, and the rattle of the elevated subway tracks, the ocean breakers still roar their timeless song on the strand—right here, in the seedy heart of summer fun in New York City.

"Is this the best beach you've ever been to, or what?" I ask eagerly, popping another shrimp into my mouth.

"Or what," Dane laughs. "The best beach I've ever been to was in Oregon. Have you ever been there?"

"No," I admit. "I've barely been anywhere. My parents like the southwest too much to leave, so growing up was a lot of camping in various rocky or sandy places. Long weekends at national forests, that kind of thing."

"Sounds rough for a girl who loves flowers."

"It might be why I love them so much. And why I came east," I add, laughing.

"My parents are both lawyers back in Indy," Dane says. "We had a week at Christmas and a week at summer; the rest of the time they were working."

"Did they want you to be a lawyer, too?"

"Of course they did." He chuckles and then sighs. "They'll keep asking me if I'm going to go to law school for a few more years, I guess, and then they'll lay off. I didn't know what I wanted to do with my life, still don't, but I know it's not law. And I like working in PR...at least, so far. What about you? Did your parents get excited when you became a landscaper?"

"Definitely not." I pause, remembering my mother's disappointed face, my father's slow shake of his head when I told them I'd chosen the local vocational school. Fortunately a group of loud kids chooses that minute to run past us on the beach below, dragging a kite behind them, and their happy shouts lighten the mood considerably. I take a long sip of my lemonade before continuing. "It wasn't what they expected for me at all. But growing things is in my blood. I *have* to do it."

Dane puts his arm around me, and I swear there are bubbles of champagne popping in my blood. I want to snuggle with this man on this park bench forever; I want this evening to stretch on and on until the end of time. "You're lucky to know why you're here," he says gently. "I hope someday I'm as lucky as you."

I hope anyone, anyone at all, can be as lucky as I am right now.

And as the moon slowly rises over the Atlantic, fireworks begin to light up the sky overhead. Coney Island is wonderful, I think.

And so is Dane.

Faking it is so working out.

On the hottest days of summer, we pick museums for our touristing. The marble halls are cool, and even the busiest draws like the Met and the Museum of Natural History offer plenty of empty galleries and forgotten exhibits, where the only people to disturb our whispers and giggles are lost tourists looking for the restrooms.

Somewhere deep within the Museum of Natural History, in a strange little room painted robin's-egg-blue and lined with glass cases full of taxidermy birds, we sit on a hard wooden bench and murmur secrets. Dane tells me that he had always wanted to learn to play guitar and now that he has some decent money coming in, he's ready to take lessons, but he's embarrassed to set it up because learning guitar is such a twelve-year-old thing to do.

I tell Dane that not only can I play the guitar, I would be happy to teach him.

"For free?" he asks, winking.

"For *double*," I correct him, "because you should have learned when you were twelve! Next time, think ahead!"

He tugs me close and our tussling quickly turns to kissing. I hear scuffled footsteps in the corridor outside and know that some wandering tourist has happened upon us, but I'm too deliriously happy to care.

Nothing matters but us.

"This garden is beautiful," Dane announces. "That's why Bashful wants to pee on it every single morning."

I look up from the flower-bed where I've been digging all morning and gave Bashful's inquiring nose a boop. "Makes sense that she likes it so much! This is a garden for children, and she's basically a toddler."

Dane looks over my garden. It's a Friday at lunchtime, but his office is closed, one of those Manhattan places where the successful leave early on Friday afternoons and no one bothers to show up in person. Dane's given his dog walker the day off, opting to bring Bashful to the park to shadow me for a few hours. I'm usually happiest working alone, but I would never turn down their company.

Dane seems to be struggling with the concept of a children's garden as opposed to an adult one, so I point out the geometric patterns and shapes I'm forming with bright blooms.

"Kids love shouting out shapes," I explain. "They love recognizing things."

"You know a lot about kids," Dane remarks, sounding impressed.

"Not really. I just work around them a lot. Near playgrounds, sidewalks where they're running by. Margot's the kid expert."

"You should work with her on one of her projects, y'know? Combo mural and garden?"

"It's funny you say that." I slowly straighten up, brushing dirt from my knees. "She wants me to do that in August, but I can't."

"Why not? It sounds so cool."

I sigh and pat Bashful, who pants up at me in ecstasy. How to explain that kids hate being forgotten? I could never remember the names of twenty-odd kids running around me once a week, to say nothing of their individual likes and dislikes and personal histories. I'd only hurt a lot of cute little feelings. "It's just not the right time," I say finally.

"Okay." Dane shrugs, accepting my answer. He looks up and down the pathway. "Sure is quiet right now," he says, grinning. "Is it the right time for a big old kiss while you're on the clock?"

I laugh and nod, stepping close to him with my dirty hands held out to the side. "I think we can get away with it."

We've been skipping Pizza Saturdays in favor of running around the city on our own, but Margot finally gets on my case about it, so on the last weekend in June, we finally take the subway down to the Lower East Side to meet my friends.

Our friends, I remind myself. They're Dane's friends, too.

I've been skating around the uncomfortable reality that I don't know how Dane joined our circle of friends. But now that we're all going to be together for dinner, it's impossible to ignore, and a familiar twist of uncertainty coils in my gut. Dane notices I'm quiet on the subway and squeezes my hand periodically, offering me comfort.

It somehow has the effect of both making me feel better and making me worry all the more.

There's a long walk from the subway station to Margot and Tracey's apartment, but instead of taking the bus, Dane suggests we walk, so we amble along the busy grid. The day is the first cool one after a week of sultry temperatures, and the evening breeze is that perfect measure of ambience, not too hot and not too cold, which only exists on the rarest and most delightful occasions. I feel myself loosening up on the stroll, enjoying Dane's company, laughing at his jokes.

We point out things we like in store windows: adult coloring books themed to classic 80s movies, an entire display devoted to LEGO figurines fighting a pitched battle between two LEGO pizza shops, a smiling fiberglass cow inviting us inside to try New York State cheese.

"I always wanted to learn to make cheese," I say, admiring the cow's pearly-whites. "I asked my parents for some goats, because I knew cows would be too much work. My high school had a really active FFA and I thought it might be fun to join. But my parents were a big no on livestock."

"That's a shame, because you would have made a cute little dairymaid," Dane teases, tickling my butt.

I smack at him and we walked on, still talking about our childhoods. I don't worry that I've told these stories before; my head is more clear than ever before. In fact, I know I'm being unusually unguarded these days, and I love it. The past few weeks have been clear successes; I can really date a guy and remember all the important stuff!

We walk past a music store and admire a vintage guitar in the window.

"Oh, you know what? I finally took my guitar in and got it tuned," Dane tells me. "So we can start any time you're ready."

"Start?" I glance at him curiously. "Start what? Oh, look, this place has all the Japanese Kit Kats. We should get some for the group. Margot loves this stuff."

"Start my guitar lessons," Dane persists, ignoring the colorful packages of Kit Kats. He tilts his head at me. "Remember? You were going to teach me guitar?"

"I was?" I'm not thinking clearly, or I wouldn't have said that. It's the ultimate giveaway of a misfiring memory. If I don't police myself against this phrase, I'd say it so often, people would definitely start to wonder what's going on with me.

But I'm still thinking about Kit Kats and who would like which flavor.

I'm still thinking about the story Dane just told me about starting a lemonade stand in his front yard—his lawyer parents made every customer sign a waiver in case he accidentally poisoned someone.

I'm still thinking about the perfect evening we're having and the warmth of Dane's hand.

I'm still thinking that I'm in love with this guy and wondering when it's safe to talk about it with him, or if it's a declaration I'm going to keep to myself for months to come.

I'm on some other planet, a planet of blissful dating happiness, lulled into security by a nice guy at my side, a gentle air temperature blessing my skin, and the prospect of pizza with my friends in just two more blocks.

If I'd been thinking clearly just now, if I'd been my normal self, I would have agreed with him about the guitar lessons and made a mental note to be better about recording promises I'd made, however casual they'd probably seemed at the time. I would give myself a stern mental talking-to about keeping up with even the tiniest, most innocuous events now that I was in a serious relationship. This is just like a job, I'd tell myself. There are expectations.

But I don't do any of that. I just look at him expectantly, waiting for him to fill me.

Dane is gazing at me like he's just discovered new and strange. Slowly, he asks, "You really don't remember, do you? When we were in Coney Island, right before the fireworks started."

"I guess I forgot," I say lamely. "It was a big night. We met a seagull!"

He tilts his head at me, and I know what's happening in that friendly brain of his.

He's calling up every mistake I've made, every conversation I've forgotten, every friendly barista or server or hot dog vendor I haven't remembered when they've given me a big, welcoming greeting. And I can't defend myself against any of these moments, because he's the only one who remembers them.

Who knows what else I've flubbed? There could be dozens of instances crowding his brain right now, odd moments where I behaved just a little too distant or a tad too confused, former coincidences that are suddenly connecting for him.

"Maeve, I—" He pauses, giving me a conflicted look.

I'm just toying with the idea of giving him a huge, smacking kiss to distract him when Caitlyn strolls up beside us, her arms full of fruit.

"Hi guys," she says brightly, missing our awkward vibe. "Look at this! A sidewalk vendor was heading home for the night and gave me everything for a dollar each. I've got blueberries, kiwis, strawberries..." She ticks off a half-dozen varieties of fruit.

"It's *Pizza* Saturday," I remind her with a grin. I've never been so thankful for an interruption in my entire life. At least, I don't think I have been. "Not Healthy Fruit Saturday."

"I'm still a vegan," Caitlyn retort. "For another week, anyway. Then my gig with the production company ends and I don't have anything lined up. I won't be able to afford to be vegan until the next job. Gotta enjoy it while I can."

She starts walking, and we fell into step beside her, listening to her discuss her various attempts to get a paying job in broadcasting. I wait a block before I reach out and take Dane's hand. He wraps his fingers around mine, and I know this near-argument was already forgotten...but I'll have to do better.

Chapter Thirteen

"I'VE NEVER EATEN so much in my entire life," I moan as we wait for the bus in City Island. "I thought I understood Italian food, but City Island has changed me."

"It changed me, too," Dane says happily, patting his stomach. "I've gone up two sizes since we got here. I blame the calamari."

"I blame the second piece of cannoli," I tell him, with a sidelong smile. He ate like a horse all afternoon as we roved around the seaside enclave, popping into cupcake shops and mom-and-pop style eateries, picking up snacks for the stroll as if we weren't planning on lobster rolls for a late lunch. He'd even brought along a literal checklist of food to try. I'd been eager to check out the nautical museum and the beautiful turreted Victorian that became the inspiration for the house in *The Royal*

Tenenbaums, but Dane had been thinking with his stomach all day.

Consequently, we'd *both* eaten way too much.

A cool breeze puffs its way up the street from the waterfront, the first dip in temperature I've felt all day. I turn my face towards it as Dane asks me, "What was your favorite part of City Island? Besides the Royal Tenenbaum house, which I thought you were going to break into and try to claim squatter's rights on."

"I wasn't *that* bad."

"Even the security camera looked nervous."

"So, you want my *other* favorite?" I look up and down City Island Avenue. Architecturally speaking, it's not the most charming place in the city, aside from the cute collection of wood-frame houses from the 1800s. The main road features low-slung seafood restaurants with glaring red or blue letters declaring their names, several large lots devoted to boat parts, and some commercial blocks which were *not* designed with beauty in mind. But the island is quirky, and I can appreciate that.

"I think Nail Island," I decide, nodding to a sign on an unattractive commercial block nearby. "That's a good name for a nail salon. You're castaway at sea, but you still want your nails pretty. Nail Island has your back."

"And you can also translate it as nail like, a handful of nails," Dane suggests. "In keeping with the shipyard theme. Now, I like the teal green Victorian house with the tiny wine shop practically in the front yard."

"Oh, me too," I agree enthusiastically. "The convenience plus the pop of color can't be beat."

Dane glances upwards as another gust of wind twirls litter in the gutters. "You know, I think it's going to rain. Do you want to take this wait into that coffee shop over there? I don't think this bus is coming anytime soon."

"Coffee would be great," I agree, even though it's probably the last thing my full stomach needed. The truth is, I've been wondering all afternoon how I was going to jot down the details of this day before they fade into the vault of my memory. I'll remember some of it on my own, but not all of it. The journal still does some heavy lifting. Plus, I'll probably fall asleep on the long bus ride back to the subway, and sleep is never a good thing when I'm trying to remember something.

And from the subway, we're going straight back to Dane's place. I love his apartment, which isn't exactly modernized but does have a fully operational air conditioner in the living room; however, the destination means I won't have a moment to myself to write anything down.

My notebook's in my bag, and my fingers are already itching to pull it out and make notes without Dane's gaze falling onto the pages. I'd been thinking of making a note on my phone once we settled onto the bus, but I know seat mates can rarely avoid glancing at what their traveling companion is doing on their phone.

Sitting at a table in a cafe will be the perfect answer. Dane can get us drinks, and when he comes back, I'll be scribbling away. I'll pretend it's a poem about the fishing boats or something. It will all appear very organic.

Thanks, rain, I mouth silently as we run across the street, swooping through the blue door of a cute little cafe just ahead of the raindrops.

"Oh, this is nice!" I exclaim as Dane closes the door behind us. Rain rattles on the plate-glass windows and the afternoon suddenly goes dark, but inside is cheerful with white walls, bright artwork, and chandeliers of old-fashioned light-bulbs hanging from ropes. "Very cool nautical vibe," I add, taking in those excellent light fixtures. I'll have to write about them, too. They're worth remembering.

"Really cool," Dane agrees. "Hey, you grab a seat and I'll get you a drink."

"Thanks!" I'm so used to not ordering my drinks, I don't think to ask him for anything in particular. I just slide into a snug little seat near the back of the cafe and pull out my notebook and pen, ready to jot down the high points of the day.

I'm busy scribbling when footsteps stop near the table. I glance up; an unfamiliar man is standing by me, face lit up in a way which always made me super uncomfortable. It doesn't happen often, but when it does, the cause is obvious.

This guy recognizes me.

And I don't recognize him.

"Hey! It's—it's Maeve, right? This is crazy!"

He pushes up the sleeves of his plaid shirt, revealing a curving tattoo on one arm. The artwork stirs a flicker of memory. "Hi," I say cautiously, dragging my eyes back to his face. Nothing there registers as familiar. *Come on, brain.* "I—um—what are the chances?"

"I know, right?" The guy looks up and down the cafe. "Did you just come up here sightseeing, too?"

"Yeah, you know...summer vacation!" I laugh. It seems a little too high-pitched. My eyes drift back to the tattoo. If he'd just push his sleeves up above his elbow, I can see what it is. And then maybe I'll remember this guy.

Before things get very awkward.

He sees my eyes wandering and grins. "Oh, remember Sheila? She's still going strong."

Sheila. A pet, maybe? A dog, or a cat, or a snake...he looks like he could have a pet snake. I'm against them by any means, but I feel like I'd remember one. "That's...good," I falter. "Well, I guess I'd better—" I gesture to my notebook. "Just have to get some things down, sorry."

"Oh, are you back in school? That's super. Sorry, I didn't mean to interrupt you. I was just so surprised—Hey, man." This is to Dane, who has appeared at his elbow with two paper cups. "Dude, I was just catching up with Maeve here. How are ya? I'm Robbie."

Robbie. Did I ever know any Robbies? With something named Sheila as a pet...or...maybe the tattoo was named Sheila. *Push up your sleeve, man!*

Dane hands me my cup. Is it me, or are his movements a little stiff? *Oh, don't be jealous, Dane! Not now, when we've had such a good day!* "Nice to meet you, Robbie," he says. "How do you two know each other?"

This is the big lie of New York City: that you can disappear. New York City, where there are millions and millions of people, so you don't *have* to bump into people you might have met and forgotten, where there are always *new* people taking their places. New York City, where I can be anonymous, not a crazy person who forgets a person as soon as she looks away from them. If only!

The awful truth is that similar people share similar interests in things like cafes and record stores and parks and historical markers, and so I do run into people I've forgotten—not all the time, but enough.

And of course, Dane, but that's different, isn't it? All those chance meetings we've had weren't really chance, they were fate. It doesn't matter that I don't remember where and when we met, because we were meant to find each other.

Right?

Robbie and Dane are both looking at me; I guess it's my privilege as the woman to tell the story in a way which won't upset my current boyfriend with any men from my past. It is Robbie's right to be painted in positive colors, and Dane's right to consider himself superior, and my right to control the narrative.

My cheeks go hot. I have absolutely nothing to say.

Dane takes in my flaming-red cheeks and I watch his jaw tighten ever so slightly.

"It was at the park last year," Robbie says finally. "Remember? At the backyard gardening expo? I presented on bromeliads."

"Oh, my God." Without thinking, I stand up and pushed his sleeve just past the elbow. A gorgeous orchid blooms on his bicep. There it is, everything I have ever known about Robbie, gleaming fresh and new in my brain. "Sheila! Your rare orchid."

"Yeah," Robbie agrees, "that's Sheila. Did you—did you forget us?" His smile is crooked, like he doesn't want to show that I've hurt his feelings.

I look between the two men, Robbie's confused face and Dane's closed one. "I...forget things...sometimes. I just get really stressed, and—" It feels like a likely lie. I dig into it, smiling with an *I'm so silly* expression. "Zoink! There it goes! It's nothing personal. I swear!"

"Hey, I understand." Robbie glances at Dane, probably realizing he's made things uncomfortable between the two of us. I see him mentally prepare to get the heck out of Dodge. "It's no problem. That was one weekend. Look, I better get going. Nice seeing you!"

Dane sits down at the table as Robbie took off. He doesn't say anything.

After a moment of wondering what comes next, I sit down across from him.

There is silence all around us.

I pick up my cup. "Wonder what you got me," I say, trying to be upbeat.

"This keeps happening." Dane drums his fingers on the table. "I tried not to notice, but I swear, every time we go out, this happens."

I'm only partially faking confusion when I ask, "What? What keeps happening?"

"We keep running into guys who act like they know you," Dane says impatiently. "You haven't noticed?"

I stare at him. I *haven't* noticed. Or, more likely, I haven't remembered. But it can't be as bad as he's making it out to be. I wave my hand dismissively and say, "Oh, it doesn't happen *that* often."

Dane snorts. "Are you kidding? In the past month, we have run into five different guys who acted like you were old friends. You always greet them like they are, too. But until today, you've never told me anything about who they are, or where you met, and Maeve, do you know how that makes me feel?"

"How?" I whisper, my fingers pressing dangerously against my paper cup. The lid threatens to pop off. I push it back into place, grateful for a distraction.

"Forgettable," Dane answers. "Like someday I'm going to be one of those guys. Just someone you used to know on the street, but not important enough to remember anymore."

"That's not why people forget things," I tell him. "It's not that simple."

"So you're not denying it, you're saying it could happen." Dane sighs and shakes his head, and suddenly I feel his impatience. He wants to leave. For the first time, one of our wonderful city dates has gone sour. "I could be one of these guys someday."

"No, of course not, Dane. I couldn't forget about you. Why are we even talking like this?" I take a sip of my drink and nearly choked. "Oh, my God. What *is* this?"

He stares at me. "It's your drink. It's a white chocolate latte with strawberry syrup and whipped cream."

"That's not a drink, that's a sundae," I grumble. "When did I tell you this was my drink?"

"You didn't," he says. "Mario made one for you last week, and you told him this was your new favorite. He said as soon as he came back from vacation he was going to make you one every single day, and you said your hips couldn't take it...but I figured today was special..."

"Oh, no." I remember the moment now. "I was just being nice. It tastes like someone dropped a cup of coffee on a birthday cake. I was hoping while he was on vacation he'd forget all about it."

At the word *forget,* Dane's face darkens again. "Not everyone just forgets things that matter to them," Dane says. "Like friendship, or dates, or secret recipes. Or offering to teach someone something that is pretty special to that person. Some people take the effort to *remember things.*"

I bite at my lip. Pretty certain his experience in life is the only experience, isn't he? Typical for a guy who has a fully operational brain to think everyone around him does, too. I'm conveniently forgetting that I've been working strenuously to give that impression as long as we've known each other. His tone puts my back up, and I'm not in the mood to pat him on the back and tell him he's unforgettable.

Especially when the truth is, I've *already* forgotten him once. The guilt of that, combined with his sanctimonious tone, makes it impossible for me to keep my head clear.

"Yeah, well," I say finally, "it's not always about making an effort, Dane. Sometimes there's more to it."

"I think it is," he argues, "and I think it also says a lot about how much you *really* care about people who care about you."

I can't take any more. "Do you? Is that what you think? Congratulations, Dane. You have a completely uneducated opinion about the human brain! Let's see what you've won." I stand up from the table and, without looking back, I stalk out.

Chapter Fourteen

I TAKE AN Uber I can't afford all the way back to my apartment, my mind seething with rage the whole way. There will be no need to write down the details of our day in City Island. I have the perfect emotionally traumatic moment to cement this day in my brain forever. The day a nice guy almost figured out my secret and proved he wasn't ready to deal with it.

I mean, what *was* that? Acting like remembering every aspect of a person's life wasn't just a personal choice, but a reflection of how they felt about other people? Memories aren't voluntary things. You can't just *choose* to remember some things and forget others. There are absolutely important moments in Dane's life that he has forgotten. And it doesn't mean a damn thing about the way he'd felt about the other people in those moments. I bet he doesn't remember anything about his sixth birthday party, for example. But his mother probably does, with fondness, so is his forgetfulness a reflection of his love for her? Not hardly.

"Jerk," I mutter, standing on the stoop of my building and tapping in a tip for the Uber driver before I head inside. The rain hasn't reached Eighty-first Street yet, but I can smell it on the air. I fumble for my front door key.

"Maeve! Hey, Maeve!"

Not again, I think miserably, but the person calling me isn't some mystery guy from my past, thank goodness. It's more surprising than that: Abel, dressed for a night out somewhere very south of West Eighty-first. "Dude, what are you doing up here? I thought the Upper West Side was for over-forties only, according to you."

"And I'm right," he declares, draping himself over my stoop's elegant balustrade. "But *you're* here, and a certain gentleman of the over-forty persuasion lives up here, and I thought, why not wander down lovely Maeve's boulevard and see if she's outside, struggling to open her front door..."

"It's going to rain," I warn him. "Do you want to come up?"

"Well, I'd be charmed," Abel drawls as I produce my key at last. "My hair would suffer from the rain and with my afternoon plans what they are..."

"Knock off the southern gentleman act on the way," I warn him. "I've had a rough afternoon."

"Oh, boy, drama." Abel hops through the front door, hot on my heels. "Let's go talk this out over some drinks."

He must be thinking of someone else's apartment when he suggests drinks, because all I ever keep around the kitchen is the occasional bottle of wine I pick up on clearance, and the wine shops are being stingy with their sales this summer. I finally find a dusty bottle of Kahlua behind some boxes on top of the fridge and he settles for that while I explain about the City Island incident.

"That's true," Abel remarks when I've finally finished my tale of woe. "You *do* seem to forget people."

"What do you mean?" I ask, wondering if I'm really so obvious. Maybe I'm not doing the superb job of holding it together that I always think I am.

Abel shrugs. "I can't tell you how many times I've seen someone flag you down or holler your name and you just *blank* on them. Like they know you, but you have no idea who they are. I always thought that was kinda weird."

I can't believe it. "No, that can't be true."

"It's true. Sometimes I wanted to ask you if everything was okay, but Margot and Tracey said it was probably just how you dealt with anxiety or something."

"You *talked* about it? With Margot and Tracey?"

"I mean, honey, we care about you! Of course we talk about you. And Caitlyn, too. Just like you must talk about me. I *hope*." Abel gives me a reproachful look, as if by not gossiping about him, I'm being the worst friend in the world.

He has a point, though. Of course we talk about him; all of us discuss each other when one of us isn't present. I just didn't know they were talking about my weird way of forgetting people. I thought maybe they were discussing my terrible taste in handbags, or how often I have dirt under my fingernails.

You should tell him. The voice in my head is back, and it's serious. For the first time, I think about listening. After all, if anyone understands fearing rejection for who they are, it's gotta be small-town, flamboyant, big-hearted Abel, right?

I lean over the arm of my couch and fumble in my bag. "Abel, there's something I want to tell you," I begin, and then I freeze.

The notebook isn't there.

My mind races, and with the clarity of memory granted by our fight, I can see it exactly where I left it.

Off to one side of the table at Clipper Coffee in City Island. With Dane.

"Oh, *no!*" I shove the bag back to the floor. "Oh *no, no, no!*"

Abel's eyes are round. "What on earth, honey?"

"My *notebook!* I left it—Dane has it—he's going to open it up and read it and he's going to see—"

"See what? I thought it was poetry! Oh, is it a journal? Is it *sexy?* Have you been writing down all your dirty fantasies? Honey, this can actually work in your favor. Let me tell you, one time I was seeing this airline pilot, and he was gone a lot, so I was writing down all the things I wanted to do—"

"No, Abel, I was writing down details from my days because otherwise I can't remember them," I blurt, giving away my secret in an instant. "I write everything in a notebook so it will jog my memory when I read them later. If I don't write it down, it as good as didn't happen."

Abel stares at me. "Honey—" he begins, then stops, at a loss for words.

"I know." I look at the floor, the parquet patterns winding in endless serpentines. Like my path through the city, running into the same people over and over again, insulting them without ever realizing I'd done it. "I have memory loss from an accident when I was a kid."

"And you never told us? Why wouldn't you tell your friends? We would help you with this, Maeve!"

I want to believe him, I really do. But I've spent my whole life running from the one memory I can't ever excise from my brain, of Angela Krebs turning her back on me and walking, hand in hand, with Shelby Langston, while the entire schoolyard watched my rejection in real-time. It took me a full year to find someone else to call my best friend, and I'm pretty sure I've never trusted anyone fully again.

Not Margot or Tracey or Caitlyn or Abel.

Not even Dane, although heaven knows I have wanted to.

"You can't tell anyone," I say. "No one."

Abel's jaw drops. "But, Maeve, we're your friends. This is serious."

"I know. I know it's serious. That's why I want you to keep it quiet. I—my *brain* is broken, Abel. I don't want the whole world to know I'm broken."

Abel puts his glass down. "Now, listen to me. We didn't sign up to be your friends because we thought you had some perfect little brain, Maeve Benson. We *care* about you. Do you think that could stop just because you need a little help keeping up with your life? I don't even remember what I had for breakfast this morning—"

"It's not like that, Abel," I interject, tired of that old saw. "It's not like being absent-minded or being so busy things slip your mind. I literally can't access my memories! And if this is true, if there are really people all over town who think they know me and I'm just ignoring them, or lying to them to get out of it, then that's—" I stop, because there are no words for how embarrassing, how awful, that could be.

I've thought all this time I was safely anonymous in the city, but it seems like I'd been leaving little breadcrumbs of myself all over the place. Making friends, making impressions, but not writing them down or missing those entries, and so for me, those encounters never happened.

But for others, I've left a hurtful moment of realizing Maeve Benson didn't even care enough to remember them. I choke back a sob, embarrassed beyond belief. How many people in New York City must think I'm a heartless bitch?

"Can you leave me alone tonight, Abel?" I moan, pushing my face against the sofa cushion. "I just need to deal with this on my own."

Murmuring protests, Abel presses a kiss to the back of my head and then leaves.

I wait until the door clicks closed behind him before I sit up and stare into the gathering gloom, wondering what the hell I'm going to do next.

I don't have to wonder for long.

Dane texts me about an hour later, while I'm moodily skimming through my menu drawer and trying to decide if I actually want dinner. His message is short and to the point.

Your notebook is at the Cafe & Croissant behind the counter. Tilda promised to leave a note for Margot about it.

I look at the text and sniffle, already on the verge of tears again. That's it, then. He's seen my notebook and realized I'd been lying to him all this time. No poems, no journal entries. Just bullet points and the facts, laid out in emotionless black and white, detailing moments from my day. I can even picture what I'd have written about today:

- long bus ride to City Island with Dane

- nautical museum, neat displays about fishing boats, very cute wooden frame houses

- the royal tenenbaums house!!

- tried out lobster roll, lemon drop cupcake, Oreo cannoli (not great), awful white chocolate strawberry latte at cute Clipper Coffee

- fight with Dane about running into random strangers who claim they know me (not great)

- let Abel up randomly and admit everything, swear him to secrecy.

- cry alone on my couch

A full day, really.

But aside from the theoretical stuff, what would he actually have seen in my notebook? I'm afraid of what he must think of my entries about our dates, our lovely times together reduced to a couple of short lines: *went for walk in park and to Gray's Papaya, saw a street artist drawing a unicorn, went back to Dane's place.* Hardly what he'd expect for a diary entry from some captivated female. It would look more like I was taking notes for an article on modern dating or something.

And now, of course, I feel like I *have* to write down what happened today. It's basically a compulsion at this point.

But my notebook is at Cafe & Croissant, and I can't just start a new one. It would be out of order and that would destroy my entire system.

A system that *works,* even if it turns out it isn't as foolproof as I once thought.

I settle for the back of a pizza place menu and grab a pen. Just a few details, to make sure I have everything straight. Then I just go to bed without bothering to order any food.

I'm not hungry.

Chapter Fifteen

MARGOT SLIDES MY notebook across the counter. It has a rubber band around it, one I hadn't put there.

"I don't know anything about it," she tells me, before I can say anything. "Tilda left a note saying you'd want to pick it up this morning. Left it somewhere?"

"With Dane, in City Island," I sigh. The cafe is still dim; Margot usually only turns on half the lights, saying a fully lit cafe before seven a.m. is inhumane. This morning, I think she's right. I'm not ready to face the bright lights of this city, and if the sun could simply not rise this morning, that would be great. I slump across the counter and blink up at Margot. "We had a fight, and I walked out. I didn't realize my notebook was sitting on the table."

"You fought with Dane? Lovely sweet Dane? Oh, Maeve. What about?" She starts up the espresso machine. "Tell me it was nothing or I'll make you something so vile you won't even want to write it down in your precious notebook."

"It was—nothing."

She lifts an eyebrow at the pause, but puts some mocha syrup into my cup, anyway. I guessed I passed the test, although hardly with flying colors.

I shrug. There's no way to tell her about the fight without giving up my secret. And I can only hope Abel is planning on keeping it from her, as requested. But as the espresso machine hums in preparation for its vital work, I can't help but ask, "Margot, have you ever noticed me, um, forgetting people? Like strangers who act like they know me?"

"Oh, *yes.*" Margot puts down the milk and nods emphatically at me. "I've always wanted to ask you about that, but it just seemed...I don't know...like the answer was going to be very confusing. Like maybe you have a secret life as a fetishist or a dungeon mistress and these are indiscreet clients you have to punish later."

"What?"

"I mean, it makes perfect sense. So like, some of them are being forgetful for real, so you just give them a couple whacks with the riding crop, but then a few are doing it on purpose, so you'll really tie them up and let them have it..." Margot trails off. "Wrong? Something else?"

"Yes, Margot, it's something else!" I hesitate. My secret is on the tip of my tongue.

"Well, Maeve, it's not like you just forget everyone you meet —" She starts to pour milk into a cup, then stops moving altogether and stares at me. Milk drips from the carton, making a tiny *plop* in the cup. It's the only noise in the room.

I drop my gaze to the counter, feeling my fingers intertwining, wringing the bones together until they hurt. The pain is the only thing that can stop me from blurting it all out, and watching my friendships slowly dry up and disappear.

Oh, if only I hadn't gotten involved with Dane! I *knew,* and I just did it, anyway. How could I be so stupid? So unguarded? So heedless of every failed friendship and relationship that had come before?

At last Margot finishes making my drink, her brow furrowed over her work. She slides the cup across the counter to me and studies my face for a moment. "Maeve, you poor thing, you really do seem to forget everyone you meet. Why is that?"

I shake my head. "No, I don't."

It was the wrong thing to do. Margot doesn't take kindly to being lied to.

I watch her sympathetic expression change to suspicion, and she suddenly grabs my notebook, drags it back across the counter, and flicks it open to a random page.

My breath catches, but I can't stop her. So I just wait.

I watch her fingers run down the page, tapping the bullet points. I can tell she's found an entry from a day in April where nothing in particular had happened: *orange vanilla latte by Mario, worked on spring planting by carousel, ordered salad for dinner from Green Goddess Cafe.* She flips the page and reads aloud in a low voice. "Went out with Margot, Tracey, Caitlyn, Abel to Film Forum. Had popcorn and watched *Dirty Dancing.* No one could believe I'd never seen it before. Went to Veselka, had the borscht. Home at midnight, straight to bed. Don't forget: bring cookies to Pizza Saturday."

Another page flips.

"Train to Grand Central to see the market, looked at fancy olive oil stand for Christmas presents. Too expensive, figure out something else. Loud thunderstorm around nine."

This is not a diary. Anyone can tell it's something else. A strange, passionless recording of events.

Margot looks at a few more entries, and a silence stretches between us.

"Maeve," she says at last, "Maeve, do you have a memory disorder?"

I don't know how she did it, but by the end of the day, Margot has me ready to confess my memory problems to our entire family of friends. Well, *ready* is a strong word. But she certainly has me convinced there is no going forward without being honest.

"And you will accept our love and support," she tells me firmly, standing over me as I dig pointlessly deep holes in a flower-bed near the Conservatory Water. "We're your *family* now. You can't expect to keep us at arm's length when we could be helping you!"

I pause in my digging and look up at Margot. She shifts her weight; she's been on her feet all day. I should tell her to go home. Just go down to the Fifth Avenue station, climb into a nice, cool train car, and snooze her way back to the Lower East Side. She doesn't have to stand here and force all her love on me.

But wow, I am so freaking thankful she's willing to do it. And that's what finally pushes me over the edge. I *have* to accept, or poor Margot will stand here for the rest of my shift, and then probably trail me home, all the way across the park, back up Eighty-sixth Street...straight to my block, by the way. I won't be walking down Eighty-fifth Street. Never again.

That is one promise to myself I *know* I'll have no problem remembering. Because he isn't going to want to speak to me, and I won't be able to bear the rejection.

Not again, and not from Dane.

I straighten and brush dirt off my knees. "Margot," I begin, then pause as a small girl runs by, shrieking, and launches herself into the pack of kids playing on the Alice in Wonderland statue. "Margot," I start again, "I give in. When should I tell everyone? I don't even know how to begin."

"I can tell them," Margot offers. "You don't have to do it. I'll explain everything."

"No, that doesn't seem right. I lied to you guys."

"You had your reasons." She's come around to some of my views as we argued all day. Margot now knows that I've lost friends over this before. But she's adamant that isn't going to happen with any of us.

I'm out of reasons to disbelieve her.

"Still, no one's going to be happy about it. Should we—get dinner, maybe?"

"Yes." Margot claps her hands. "We'll do it on Pizza Saturday. I'm not working at the cafe on Saturday morning, by the way. I have a meeting to finalize the mural."

"Margot!" I forget my own misery for a moment. "The community board finally accepted the concept?"

"They sure did." Margot's smile could light up the whole world. "I have no idea how I'm going to do this entire thing by myself, but I got it. You know I could still really use your help with the garden in front, right?"

I kick at the dirt. "I know."

Margot leans in and hugs me, not even wrinkling her nose at my sweaty, dirty self. "Stop letting your fears stop you, honey. This could be a wonderful chance to reset, okay? You don't have to do everything by yourself. You've got *us*."

Everyone cries, but no one cries as hard as me.

Okay, that's a lie. Abel cries the hardest.

But he's just doing it because he's theatrical and loves a good reason to sob in front of other people. Meanwhile, I'm across the living room crying because I'm so embarrassed and afraid. Margot is crying because she's proud of herself for bringing me back into the fold and accepting their love and support. Tracey is crying because she is an emotional mess who cries at everything, as much as she tries to hide it. Caitlyn is crying in polite little sniffles, dabbing at a few errant tears, but I know that means as much, or more, than Abel's huge bellowing sobs. Caitlyn doesn't let her emotions run away with her. She doesn't even let them go out for short walks.

When we've gotten through all the weeping and hugging and watery laughter that comes after a big emotional outburst, Margot claps her hands for attention.

"You have to stop doing that," Abel complains. "We are not your first graders."

"When you stop *acting* like a first grader," Margot begins, looking stern, but Tracey cuts her off.

"Not this time, guys." She wipes at her eyes. "I'm too fragile to even deal with your pretend arguments."

"Oh, fine." Margot winks at Abel, then she turns her dazzling smile on me. "Maeve, permission to spill the beans?"

"Go ahead," I sigh. There's no stopping Margot once she gets rolling, anyway.

"Maeve is going to work on the school mural project with me!" Margot announces. "She's going to lead the school kids in planting a garden that is part edible, part just beautiful, underneath the mural. So in spring when everything is blooming, the mural will spill into the garden. All the same colors. From paint to flowers, see?" She holds up her phone and everyone *ooh*s at the thumbnail-sized concept art she'd used to get the project approved.

"That's the idea, anyway," I say modestly, but everyone is already congratulating us on the incredible design, as if we've done the hard work ahead of us, and the mural/garden is already in full bloom.

Margot is jubilant and in her element, having won the day on multiple fronts, but I feel utterly wrung out. I head back to the kitchen island to pour myself another drink, and Tracey joins me. She gives my shoulder a little squeeze. "I'm so sorry we didn't see you were struggling with your memory," she whispers. "Thank you for telling us. Now we can help you."

"It's really okay," I begin. "You don't need to help..."

"No one should have to struggle with something like that on their own," she interrupts. "You're part of our family, Maeve. Let us be there for you, okay?"

"Okay," I agree, and a little weight seems to slip from my shoulders.

"As for Dane..."

Oh, there's that weight I was missing! That wasn't gone long.

"We told him we were canceling Pizza Saturday this week," Tracey says.

"Yeah, Margot told me you were doing that. It was nice of you. I don't expect you to always...I guess we can sort of take it slow—" I don't know how to handle the split-up when we all hang out together. This is why you shouldn't date in your friend pool.

The thing is, though, I forgot he was in my friend pool.

I still don't know exactly how that happened. I wonder if I'll ever figure it out. Probably I should just let it go...

"But I still think you should tell him," Tracey is saying.

"About skipping Pizza—"

"About your *memory*," Tracey corrects me. "Because Dane is our friend, too. But more importantly, because you two are a good couple, and you shouldn't break up over this. You can work this out, girl! You just need to communicate."

I draw a deep breath to stop any errant tears from showing up. "Tracey, *he* hasn't called me. I don't think you should be telling *me* that we shouldn't break up. This isn't my decision." It's so much easier to blame him, I actually believe myself.

Tracey doesn't buy it. "I'm sorry, Maeve, but...didn't *you* walk out on him in City Island?"

I hesitate, realizing she has me, and Tracey's face immediately clouds with regret. "Oh, I'm sorry," she gasps. "I—do you—remember what happened that afternoon?"

"I remember," I assure her hastily. "Something like that, you don't forget. Not even with a broken brain like mine."

I remember all of it, as fresh and painful as the day it happened. But that will fade, right?

Tracey takes a fresh bottle of Coke out of the fridge and puts it on the kitchen island, ready to top off everyone's drinks. Abel stops sniffling and looks up—he's off his seltzer craze and Tracey knows it. She's such a good mom to us in so many ways. I guess there is always a mom of the group...and a problem child of the group, which we probably used to think was Abel, but which had clearly been my title all along.

And Dane? Since he joined the group, he's been nothing but wonderful. And apparently, he's part of the original line-up. The nice guy. The handsome one with a good job who just hasn't met the right person yet. The one I could have had, if I'd just worked a little harder.

But, that's not true, is it?

I lied to Dane by keeping him in the dark about my memory, by letting him think I was writing poetry instead of summarizing our days together. I lost him, fair and square, not just because I'm the freak of the group, but because I lied.

It's natural that I don't want to talk to him now.

But if my refusal to reach out to him ends up costing him these amazing friends, then I'll be behaving worse than ever.

I'm going to *have* to talk to him.

Soon. But not tonight.

Tonight, I just need to draw a few deep breaths and get used to a world where my friends know my secret, and they haven't run away from it.

Chapter Sixteen

NOT TONIGHT TURNS into not this weekend, then not this *week,* pretty quickly.

There are always plenty of excuses: first there is the Fourth of July—the city is crazy, people are going out of town for parties, everyone's schedules are upended for the holiday weekend. The next Pizza Saturday is canceled so that Margot, Tracey, and Abel can go back home for the weekend; they insist there is no place like a tiny midwestern town for celebrating Independence Day, and vow that next year I am coming back with them.

Suddenly, it's mid-July, and people are back, but there are new excuses to avoid Dane. Summer concerts in the park mean I spend extra hours at work, cleaning up messes left by crowds, and I have to cover vacation time for the more senior landscapers. And then the mural and garden project arrives, just in time to fill six weekends of city kids' summer vacation. I still can't believe I agreed to do it. And yet here I am, putting on my garden clothes, about to face a hot, humid Saturday morning and Margot's unstoppable enthusiasm for art.

And kids I don't know.

Margot is waiting at the little park next to a brick school building on the Lower East Side. She's got iced coffees —"Nothing fancy, since I didn't make them myself," she insists, but there's something marvelous about mine.

"Seriously, Margot, what *is* this?"

"Oh, an orange-vanilla syrup. I wasn't sure I'd like it. Do you?"

"Yes," I say. "I don't even mind that you experimented on me."

Margot is still laughing when our crew arrives.

Twenty adorable elementary school children, all between eight and ten, I'd say. Old enough to take directions and get their hands dirty, according to Margot.

This was the part I've been afraid of. They are all staring at me; they are all little Angela Krebs looking back at me with open, innocent faces.

None of them are aware of how badly they can hurt me. Conversely, none of them are aware that if they see me on the street tomorrow, I'll probably walk right past them without even recognizing them, without even saying hello. How would that make them feel? I have to be careful to stay away from here for a while, only come down for Sunday's gardening, then get out.

Thank goodness this isn't my neighborhood. I feel lucky to be entombed (Margot's word) on the Upper West Side, where it's unlikely I'll run into any of these smiling little angels during the week. Bad enough that I'm letting down adults by forgetting them; letting down children in this way would just feel villainous.

Of course, kids *do* go to my part of town all the time. But before I can panic about potential meetings in Central Park or while passing by the steps outside the Museum of Natural History, Margot steps in and sets their expectations at a realistic level. She makes the introductions, then claps her hands to signify she really needs their attention.

They gaze at her, enraptured.

"Maeve has a short-term memory disorder, everyone," she declares.

I cringe, but Margot plows on.

"Do we know anyone with memories that do funny things?"

A girl in the front row raises a tentative hand. "My grandma," she volunteers. "Sometimes she thinks I'm her little sister from olden times."

"There you go. That totally sucks, but it's not her fault, right?"

The little girl shakes her head. A few others join in. Presumably, they all have loved ones with dementia. I wasn't quite sure that was the connection I would have liked them to make, but...

"So it's not *quite* like that for Maeve," Margot goes on, clarifying her point. "The good news is, she can get to her missing memories with a little help. She just needs a special reminder. So I was thinking, maybe we could do a secret hand sign? And then if we see Maeve out in the city, we can do our secret hand-sign and she'll know we're garden buddies. Want to do that, guys?"

The kids nod so eagerly, I feel tears spring to my eyes. I've been pretty weepy lately, but this time? These tears actually feel really good.

With Margot's supervision (to make sure nothing lewd or racist creeps in by accident) the kids devise their garden buddies hand-sign: a series of thumbs-up and crossed fingers and two claps. Everyone practices until they have it, me included. There is so much laughter in the process, I know that even if I forget these kids for a night or two, I'll never forget the secret signal... or the fun we had coming up with it.

After we've gone through the hand-signs and divided up kids between those who want to garden and those who want to paint, I set up the kids to mark out the garden according to my plans. Once they're busy, I walk over to Margot to thank her. She's helping her group understand the grid they're going to use while drawing the mural design onto the school wall.

"That's it, Jose. You just follow the same lines you see on the paper—just make them on the wall with chalk and then I'll paint them in. After *that,* we can start filling in the blocks with paint. Go for it!" Margot sends the kids off with their chalk and turns to me. "So that was fun, huh?"

"How did you think of making up a sign? It was genius."

"Tracey's idea, actually. You know she has a cousin who is deaf, right? So Tracey knows a little sign-language. When they were kids, they had a few secret signs to get around her cousin's parents and anyone else who might know ASL." Margot grins. "She realized that a secret sign could help you figure out you know a person even if you're not sure where from. It won't cure everything, but it'll help with those awkward moments on the street. I know you were dreading disappointing a fourth-grader, and now you don't have to."

"This is incredible." I watch the kids playing in the dirt. "I wish something like this could help me with everyone else I meet. Do you think we could convince people our age to flash me a sign?"

Margot wraps a comforting arm around my shoulders. "We'll figure something out," she says. "You're not in this alone anymore."

I know I'm not, but it still feels like I am, a little bit. Tonight is the first Pizza Saturday in weeks, and I was supposed to have told Tracey by now if I was on speaking terms with Dane.

I'm not, and I don't know how to admit it.

I guess I don't even want it to be true.

I want Dane back in my life, but after a month of silence between us, that seems pretty unlikely. And it's on me: I picked the fight; I kept a secret from him; I didn't trust him to stick around. But is that so crazy?

I mean, seriously. There are a million stick-figure women with big boobs and fully operational brains in this city—why would he waste his time pining over someone like me? He probably doesn't even want to come to Pizza Saturday. He'd probably just cede our friendship family back to us, letting us go as easily as he'd found us, to avoid facing me.

Or maybe he had already forgotten me and the rest of the gang. Maybe whatever had brought us together really had been forgettable, even for a normal person.

Maybe that has been the problem all along.

Maybe the weekend we met wasn't worth remembering, and everything that came after hadn't been fate. It had been chance: the random chance of a pinball rattling through a city, banging off bumpers, while a toddler was merrily pressing buttons without strategy or thought.

Yeah, that makes more sense.

I look around for a distraction. Anything to get past this constant rehashing of the events of the first half of the summer. Just forget it, Maeve. Like you forget everything else.

A girl leaning over the planter beckons to me, her eyes bright over some find she's made in the fresh soil, and I head over to help her. I have an idea of her name, like a little seed of my own.

"Let me see that, um, is it Monique? Moni-*qua*," I correct myself, and the girl laughs.

"It's Monesha," she says, not at all offended. "You were so close! Hey, look at this worm. Isn't she cool?"

Chapter Seventeen

Two hours later, parents and caretakers show up to escort their grubby children home, and Margot and I plop ourselves down on the planter and stare at each other. There really aren't words for how tiring this morning was. So *many* kids! Margot does this every day during the school year, too. Class after class of tiny art students. She's a wonder.

"That was a lot," I say finally. "I'm wiped out."

Margot wipes some chalk dust from her jeans. "It was amazing, though, right?"

I think about all those kids, their glee as they dug through the potting soil and ran strings around plots to designate where their blooms would go. "It was amazing," I admit. "I'm so used to gardening alone while people's kids run around in the background. I've never even thought about teaching kids how to make things grow. It feels really good. Tiring, but good."

"I'm so glad you're doing this with me," Margot says. "Seriously. Thank you. I could never have done the gardening part myself."

"Thanks for not giving up on me," I reply softly.

"I would never give up on you," Margot informs me. "You're my *friend*. That word means something, Maeve! If you can only remember one thing, remember that."

She slips away from my side and begins picking up the discarded chalks and rolls of string left around our work area. I resolve to join her, closing my eyes as if that will help me dig up the energy. I'm pretty sure this morning's gardening club was the most socially active thing I've done since childhood, and I'm exhausted inside and out.

When I open my eyes, I see Dane standing in front of me.

I close them tight again, *squeezing* them shut. Hallucinations? It's hot, so maybe I have heat stroke. I fumble for the water bottle at my side.

"Maeve," Dane's voice says.

I open my eyes again. He's still standing there. His face concerned. He's *real*. "Are you okay? Should I—" and then his hand is on my forehead.

He's only taking my temperature, but I want to swoon dead away from his touch. I want to go full damsel in distress. I don't need water, I need smelling salts.

"Dane, what are you doing here?" I murmur. I don't trust my voice at a higher volume; it will wobble and then I'll just burst into tears.

He takes his hand away—I miss the feel immediately—and sits down next to me. "I was passing by about an hour ago and saw you in here with all these kids. I—I wanted to hang out and watch, but—" he grins ruefully. "I didn't want to be a creepy adult. Someone might call the cops. So I've been at the cafe down the street, watching for a bunch of kids to go past, so I'd know when you guys were done."

"Oh...okay." I pause, not sure where to take things from here. But one thing seems obvious. One thing I *have* to say. "Dane, I'm sorry."

"About what? Fighting with me up in City Island? Don't be. I was being a petty jerk. So you forget some things, that's not the end of the world. You don't owe me any explanations. I shouldn't have picked a fight with you."

I close my eyes. "Dane, that's nice, but there's something I need you to know."

"Not right now, okay?" Dane pulls me into his arms and I can't fight against the feeling of blessed *home* I get once I'm there.

This is going to get worse before it gets better, a voice warns me, but I let him have his way.

Margot must be annoyed I'm not helping her clean up, but if so, she doesn't say anything.

* * *

We walk to a quiet bar a few blocks away, where Bon Iver is warbling softly from a speaker on a shelf above the whiskey bottles, and the bartender is quietly typing into her phone. She gives us a small smile and pours drinks for us without speaking. I get the impression she is trying to wring every slow moment out of the midday stillness before Saturday afternoon drinkers descend.

Dane settles me into a corner table, where the air is cool and the street noise blurred. "I've been wanting to sit across from you and have a drink for the past month," he admits, his voice gravelly with emotion. "How have you been?"

"Good," I say automatically, and then wince. "Well, bad, if we're being honest. Dane, I know I over-reacted, but—"

"Not yet," he says, and it's a request.

I nod my assent.

"Thank you." Dane puts his hand over mine. "Maeve, I've been a jealous asshole."

I raise my eyebrows. "Jealous?" Of everything he might have said, that isn't what I'd expected to hear.

"Jealous," he repeats. "There's something about you that makes people *remember* you, even when they make no impression on you. The way I've seen men call to you, say your name, and you just walk on by like they don't exist. I couldn't understand it. And then I realized, I'm just the same. Ever since the weekend we met, I've been thinking about you. And when I saw you again, I had to say your name, had to get your attention...even though it was clear I hadn't made any impression on you at all."

I gasp with shock, but Dane plunges on before I can stop him and demand an explanation.

"I know you didn't spend nine months of the past year thinking about me, hoping you'd see me again, and that's okay, Maeve. It's okay. But...can I just ask...is there any chance you've spent a few days of the past month thinking about me?"

I can't help it. I burst into tears.

Dane's grip tightens on my hands. "Don't cry, Maeve, I'm so sorry—god—"

"No, it's not that." I sniffle and try to pull myself together. Dane finally relinquishes my hands and I grab my cocktail napkin, ineffectually wiping my face with the tiny scrap of paper. "Dane, I have to tell you something and you have to listen, okay? It's not—look, first off, I think I might be in love with you."

Dane's face lights up, and for a moment I'm afraid he might do something awful, like say it back.

Not now, not before I've confessed!

I plunge into my confession before he can fit a word in. "But you need to know something about me. I don't remember things, Dane. I want to, and I try to, but I just *can't*. Not without help. I have this weird condition. It makes things really hard. And Dane—" the tears are back in full force, because clearly something which had meant so much to him hadn't been enough for me, and the idea of it is breaking my heart. "Dane, I have tried and tried to figure it out, but I don't know how we met. I don't remember it at all."

His face changes—it *darkens*. There is no other word for it; one moment, his face is alight with excitement and love, then it grows dark as those emotions fade away. He seems to struggle for a moment before he says, "But—you must remember *something* about it."

"Dane," I say, brushing away the pesky tears on my cheeks, "you saw my notebook. You must see the way I—"

"I didn't open your notebook," he interrupts, his voice catching. "It's *yours,* isn't it? I put a rubber band around it so no one else would open it and I left it at the cafe, because you left in such a huff, I knew you wouldn't want to see me right away. I was just waiting for you to text me."

I close my eyes.

"But you didn't."

"I didn't think you wanted to talk to me," I whisper. "I thought you'd figure it out and you wouldn't want me anymore."

"Figure out what? That I'm just another guy to you? Just one more guy to walk past on the sidewalk? Jesus, Maeve. It's that guy from the stoop, isn't it? The one yelling to you about your date night. I guess I accidentally interrupted your social calendar that week. I tried to forget it, but now I don't know."

"What?" My eyes fly open again. "What are you talking about?"

"Before we really started dating," Dane says. "The first night I was at your apartment. I left, and I was at the corner when I heard some guy shouting at you about going out with him. You invited him up. I should have—I shrugged it off, because we kept seeing each other, but maybe—"

"That was *Todd*," I realize with horror, putting two and two together so easily, I can picture the night he's talking about. "My idiot friend Todd. We do this thing called Fake Date Night, where we dress up and go to nice restaurants. It's leftover from college. If you heard someone talking to me about a date night, that's what it was. We went to a French place on West Fiftieth, if you're curious, and it was terrible."

"Oh. Well. I see." Dane looks into his drink. "This reunion isn't going the way I hoped."

His words crush me.

Because I know it's over. We tried—Dane tried—and we're here now.

"I'm sorry." I stand up, know I have to get out of here. Have to get away from him. "I'm sorry it didn't work out."

"Maeve, wait—"

"No," I say. "It shouldn't be this hard." And I don't know if I meant admitting my problem to him, or just that we can't seem to get our stories straight with each other.

So I leave.

Chapter Eighteen

"WHERE ARE YOU?" Margot's voice is impatient; or maybe that's just how she sounds on phone calls. I'm pretty sure it's the first time she's ever made a voice call to me. "You were supposed to come over tonight! Dane is coming, remember him? Hot guy that you left with earlier, so I had to do all the clean-up?"

"I can't make it," I say, trying to sound weak and sick. It's not hard, since I've been crying all afternoon and my throat is sore from sobbing. "I got heat stroke in the park this afternoon. I have to rest."

"You did *not*. You work outside in the heat every single day. Now get your ass down to our place for Pizza Saturday. We are waiting for you."

"Waiting for me? Why would you be waiting for me?" I sit up on the sofa, suspicious. "What's going on besides pizza?"

"We're celebrating the park project, *duh*. It's a party! And you are literally one of the guests of honor, next to me. You're missing your own party? Get in a car and get down here."

I sigh and look at the slanting light outside. It's past seven o'clock. Dating hours in NYC are now in full effect. Cars are going to be expensive.

"Don't sigh," Margot warns me. "Just do it. Or I'll order one for you myself."

"Fine, don't do that," I grumble. She's impossible to fight. "I'm ordering a car. See you in twenty."

I fret all the way to the Lower East Side apartment, ignoring the attempts of my young and enthusiastic driver to be chatty. She's nice enough, obviously pleased to pick up a woman about her own age, but I just have nothing to say. What could I tell her? I broke up with my boyfriend this afternoon because I simply couldn't admit to him I had a memory disorder? Even though my friends had gone out of their way to make it obvious that not everyone in the world was as awful and self-centered as Angela Krebs had been?

I appreciate their attempts, but they just don't know what I'm going through.

A lifetime of keeping a secret isn't something a person can drop overnight. And Dane didn't make it easy for me to feel open and honest with him this afternoon.

Not when he'd just revealed he'd secretly been jealous of Todd during all those golden weeks we'd been dating.

What was I supposed to say to that? He'd thought I'd been lying about Todd, for heaven's sake.

And what was all that about people all over the city looking at me, trying to catch my eye? That didn't *happen*.

Did it?

"I really like this block," the Lyft driver says desperately, like she thinks I won't tip her without some conversation.

"There was a crime spree here last week," I lie. "Ten people were shot."

She stops talking after that.

I hop out of the car outside Tracey and Margot's building without a backward glance at the horrified driver. Then I just stand on the curb a moment, taking it all in, breathing deeply. Trying to start again.

The trees outside the brick apartment house are rocking gently in the evening breeze off the East River; the buses on the avenue half a block away are grunting and groaning along their route; a siren wails as fire trucks race to an emergency another block down. An older man is walking a beagle up the sidewalk, laughing as the dog jogs along with her nose to the pavement, following some tantalizing scent.

Remember this moment, I command myself, *just as it is, remember every detail.* Every now and then, I try this.

Every now and then, it actually works.

I glance back at the nondescript stoop of my friends' building, and blink in surprise.

Tracey is sitting on the steps, her dark hair falling over her shoulders. She's looking up the street in the opposite direction, and at first, I think she's watching the man and his beagle. Then she raises her hand in greeting, and that's when I realize Dane is walking towards us, a pizza box in his hands.

I draw in a shaky breath. *How could she invite him? How could he come?*

But suddenly, there's something else in my mind, overwhelming the shock and hurt.

Something like...a memory.

I make myself stand still, waiting for whatever comes next.

"Oh my goodness," Tracey cries as Dane approaches. "You're not Abel. I'm so sorry. You must think I'm crazy."

What?

Yes.

"No, it's fine." Dane stands by the foot of the stairs and looks up at Tracey, keys in hand. "I love this kind of thing. It's so New York, people meeting up on the block. I want this for myself, someday."

I feel my jaw dropping all on its own. *I've heard this before.*

"You can have it right now," Tracey suggests. "Since when are you our neighbor?"

"I've only been in the building a couple of days...but I have to be out by the end of the week."

"Evicted?" Tracey suggests, grinning.

"Oh, just staying on a *very* short sublet while a friend is out of town. Anthony in 5D, do you know him?"

"No, but we've only been here about a month, anyway," Tracey says.

I have to put my hand against the rough bark of the tree trunk and use it for balance, suddenly unsteady on my feet. My head is spinning.

"You going to eat that pizza alone?" Tracey goes on. "Because my roommate and I only have salad for dinner, but we could be convinced to trade some lettuce and tomato for a couple of slices. Plus, we'll throw in our amazing good company for free. We're pretty new to the city, so we're collecting new people to hang out with. A college friend is coming over, and I met a really cool chick making a movie on her phone over in Union Square. *She's* coming. And I think this girl we met at the High Line is coming over. She was playing in the flowers and we couldn't resist adopting her."

A vision fills my mind: white daisies and purple coneflowers, rocking back and forth in a breeze off the Hudson River. The High Line, crowded with walkers, rushing past me while I knelt amongst the blooms and touched their stems with fascinated fingers. I'd been so excited to find the wildflower gardens on the High Line, an elevated train track-turned-park, that I'd eagerly welcomed the first people to stop and ask me what I was doing.

The only people to stop and ask.

Margot and Tracey.

My eyes fill with tears. *That* was the day we met. How could I have forgotten?

"A film director and a flower child, huh? A tough offer to refuse," Dane says, cocking his head like he's mulling it over. "It's a pretty big pie. I think there might be enough here for six—if you and your friends don't mind extra pineapple as a topping..."

"What?" Tracey had been standing up, but now she sits right back down and puts her chin in her hands, her elbows on her knees. "Never mind. Offer rescinded. Good luck on your next apartment."

"I'm joking, I swear." Dane lifts the pizza box lid. A gust of wind rushes past him, carrying the scent of pepperoni and cheese, and the moment it hits my nostrils, I remember what comes next.

The next line is mine.

I push away from the tree and stroll up to the two of them, my hands clenched tightly behind my back so they can't see how badly I am shaking.

"Hi, guys," I announce, as boldly as I can. "Remember me? Hey Tracey, flirting with the pizza boy, really? That's fun."

Tracey squeals with delight, standing up and running down the steps to embrace me. But even as her arms wrap around me and my chin ends up on her shoulder, I can only look at Dane.

His smile, so hopeful and fragile, is the sign I need.

"Ah-ah," Tracey says, when I try to go to Dane. "That's not part of the show!"

I look at him wistfully, but he shakes his head. His smile illuminates his face. But the next line is mine.

"I thought we were having salad," I say.

"But what about pizza?" Tracey laughs. "Because this guy has pizza, and he's willing to share."

Up in the apartment, the script continues to play out, but now I know it as well as the other players. Heart full, I join in the fun.

Dane brings in the pizza, and Margot cheers and calls him a visitation from heaven. Abel comes over full of pizza excitement and manages to topple the big bowl of salad Margot had chopped up for everyone to share. Everyone reacts as if this is a huge surprise, when in reality, we all knew it was going to happen. Because it happened before.

I curl up around a pillow on the couch and mostly stay quiet, because this play is based on real life, and this is exactly what I'd done on the weekend we met. I can remember it all now with crystal-clear clarity.

I'd been my usual wallflower self, observing everything around me, making mental bullet points so I could jot them down in a notebook later.

Things look different the second time around. Now I see the very first Pizza Saturday as Dane must have, when he'd been the good-natured visitor from out of town, finding himself basking in the warmth of a circle of friends. Imagining the life he could lead for himself if he lived here full time.

But all that glancing my way he's been doing, is *that* in the script? Had he already been intrigued by the quiet girl in the corner? It sure seems that way...unless the surreptitious looks he's throwing my way tonight aren't part of the show.

When the pizza is half-gone and Caitlyn has arrived, witnessed the non-vegetarian carnage, and popped back out for what will become her traditional Saturday night California rolls, I feel myself tensing, pulling back into the sofa cushions. I know what's coming next, but I don't know what it will feel like to relive it.

This might hurt, I tell myself.

Dane comes over right on cue, holding two red plastic cups. He hands one to me, and I know before I even lift the cup to my lips that he has brought me Margot's celebrated homemade sangria. It's potent stuff, and possibly harder on my memory than anything else if I have more than one cup of it.

If I'd had two that night...well, then it would be no wonder I'd forgotten this particular Pizza Saturday, as significant as it had been in my life. No wonder there are no notes in my journals to explain the sudden introduction of Margot, Tracey, Caitlyn, Abel, the tradition of Pizza Saturday...or the come-from-afar stranger Dane, who had gone home but never forgotten me.

"So, you're the quiet one," Dane says, following the script to the letter.

"I guess I am," I reply. "Don't take it the wrong way or anything."

"How should I take it?" His smile is a smoldering promise and I know with all my heart that it had been that night, too. I just hadn't noticed; I'd never had any reason to believe a guy like Dane would see anything in a girl like me. I can see the truth now, though. Dane came back to New York and our circle of friends, not just for the camaraderie we offered...but for me.

The realization nearly makes my heart burst right out of my chest.

So, I go off script. I'd been running out of words, anyway. The sangria must have kicked in by now on this night last summer, because I'm fumbling for the memory again. It hasn't fully disappeared this time; it isn't locked away. It's simply cloudy, the memory of a girl who has had a cup of her friend's very strong sangria and doesn't yet know that her life is changing forever.

"Take it as a compliment," I tell him. "I was saving all my conversation for you."

Interest sparks in Dane's eyes. "But what if I don't want to talk to you, Maeve?"

"What do you want, then?"

He leans over me, and my heart flutters. "I want to kiss you until there's no way you could ever forget me," he whispers.

I open my mouth to joke, to say there's no fear of that. But Dane's lips are on mine, and before I can ruin this moment, he is doing his best to make sure it's one that lasts forever.

Chapter Nineteen

AUTUMN GARDENS ARE their own challenge, but I like the work that goes into making cold-hardy plants look as lush and colorful as the summer gardens. The key is to keep changing things, bringing in new plantings as the temperatures dip, surprising park regulars with new designs and fresh blooms even as the leaves fall from the trees and the park prepares to enter a long period of winter sameness.

I stand back and look over the flower beds I've just updated along the Wien Walk, a broad and busy walkway leading from Fifth Avenue to the back entrance of the Central Park Zoo. Beside me, a small acolyte from the mural garden project stands back as well, looking equally satisfied.

"You did a nice job, Mercedes," I tell her, and the small girl smiles up at me.

"Thanks for letting me garden with you, Maeve," she says. "I'm going to miss the flowers in winter, though."

"Well, that's what our Saturday group project will be this weekend," I reveal. "We're going to work on flowers you can grow all winter in your apartments. Sound good?"

"Oh, yay!" Mercedes performs a little twirl that ends up with her crashing into her mother's legs. "Sorry, Mommy!"

Mrs. Flores gives me a chuckle and a wave. She doesn't speak much English, and I have only very basic Spanish, but over the summer, we found we were able to communicate enough to arrange for Mercedes to join me for a half-hour or so on Friday afternoons in the park.

It was a simple arrangement with my supervisor to take on some volunteer hours outside of work. She'd liked the initiative of the community garden, just as Margot had promised. Adding in volunteering in the park? Even though I'm doing it because I enjoy the work, it's starting to look like I'll have management's support if I choose to apply for one of the landscape architect positions that always open in early spring.

Mercedes isn't the only one who has a standing appointment with me on the east side of the park. As Mercedes and Mrs. Flores head towards the subway, Dane rises from his usual spot a few benches away. And as usual, he pulls me close for a kiss, even as I protest I'm going to ruin his nice work clothes with my dirty ones.

"Are you ready for date night?" he asks.

"Only if it's close and they don't mind a very muddy person," I say. "Because I'm tired. And muddy, if you didn't notice. And so are you now."

"Oh, they won't mind."

"They?"

Dane smiles.

"What did you do?"

"I hope you didn't think we were going to just let our four-month anniversary slide."

"Our four-month—" I blink at him. "Are you just showing off that you're better at remembering things than me?"

"No," Dane says. "I just really like pizza."

"I am not going to go downtown at four thirty on a Friday for pizza," I tell him wearily. "I'm way too tired. Can't we just go home? To my apartment," I add, "where my shower and clean clothes are."

"Of course we can," Dane agrees. "As long as you come right back over to my place afterwards. What?" He laughs as I shoot him a suspicious look. "Bashful will want a walk."

"Bashful is out with her dog walker right now," I remind him.

"You got me," Dane says, unabashed. "Now come on, flower girl. Let's go celebrate."

He walks me home and we kiss on the stoop, getting his clothes even dirtier. Then I head upstairs, take a shower, sit down on my bed for "just a minute", and fall asleep.

I wake up an hour later to five text messages. One from Dane, one from Tracey, one from Margot, one from Abel, one from Caitlyn. All of them wondering if I am okay, with varying levels of hysteria.

Abel wants to know if I have fallen in the shower and died.

Tracey wants to know if I am sick and if so, should she bring over soup.

Margot asks if I am blowing them off because if so, she totally gets it.

Caitlyn suggests I just stay in bed until I feel up to company again.

And Dane's simply says, *Call me and I'll come get you. I love you.*

So I call him, wondering if I've forgotten some important party.

Dane shows up ten minutes later in a car, which is an extravagance I figure I will probably have to yell at him about later. I buzz him up and unlock the front door, pulling a brush through my hair with the last thirty seconds of prep time left to me. When he comes bounding in, I whirl around, anxious in case I'd forgotten something. "I'm sorry, I just don't remember making plans," I begin.

"You didn't," he promises me. "When I picked you up in the park, I said to come over to my place for dinner after you'd cleaned up."

"Oh, that's right." The entire afternoon comes back to me in a flash. I sigh, glad it isn't something bigger, but sorry my forgetfulness intervened with the evening plans. I am so careful, but something as simple as an unexpected nap can knock the last hour right out of my mind. "I must have just fallen asleep, and I forgot."

"It's fine, really. I should have texted you in case you fell asleep. I knew you were wiped out from work." Dane wraps me up in his arms and I rest my head against his shoulder. I know I'll never get tired of feeling so warm and loved.

And so understood.

He gets me; and because of that, I feel at home with him.

And with our friends.

After he partnered up with our friends to recreate the weekend we'd met, I changed my secretive ways for good. I was honest with all of them about what I remembered and what escaped me. And in return, they gave me recaps, sent me reminder messages, and took lots of photos—all things that helped my brain recall the memories it had accidentally locked away.

It's been amazing.

And Dane filled me in on everything he'd done to get back to New York City after that weekend—fueled, he explained, by a crazy need to find me again. But it hadn't been easy. He'd gotten a job in the city, but then he couldn't remember Margot and Tracey's last names. And he couldn't get into the building without knowing someone there. It had been pure chance to walk into a cafe on the Upper West Side where both Margot and I were at the same time.

"Or pure destiny," he added when he told the story.

Fate, I reminded myself. It gives me goosebumps, every time. All those moments we'd found each other, like sheer perfection for a girl who couldn't remember faces of people she'd met or plans she'd made on the fly, adding up to what we have now.

Pure happiness.

"You guys are gross," Margot tells us every time we kiss. "I regret getting you together. Both times."

"You didn't do it the second time," Tracey always tells her. "We did it as a team."

"So we're all to blame," Abel would answer.

"I'll take some of that blame," Caitlyn would say.

"It was my idea," Dane protests. "Don't I get some of the credit?"

The same script, every time.

And every time, I look at Dane, and he looks back at me, and we use the signal we'd come up with, the one to always remind me of who I'm with—as if I could forget now—a nod, a wink, a tap on the forehead, and a smile. *It's us,* that signal says. *We're us.*

Whoever's to blame for it, he and I are *us* now.

I slip on my shoes and he pauses at the door now and nods, winks. I tap my forehead and smile.

"Ready to go see our friends?" he asks. "They're in full party mode and probably destroying my apartment. Bashful will be barking. It's going to be pandemonium."

"Sounds like them," I laugh. "Sounds like a night to remember."

Sneak Peek: The Settle Down Summer

A FEW YEARS later...

Maeve's friends have grown into their lives in New York City. Tracey runs an art gallery,   Abel is an art broker, Caitlyn is working her way through a meteorology degree, and Margot is still teaching art to kids. Their lives look great on paper, but living in the city hasn't always been easy, especially in recent years. When Tracey, Caitlyn, and Margot decide they can't take another year of being single in the city, they form an alliance.

The Settle-Down Society.

They'll get married, get settled, and get *out.*

The three woman start their dating journeys on an app that Margot recommends called Lifer. And when Tracey meets Chase, she knows her journey begins and ends with him.

But is Chase really her soulmate?

Or is there someone else in Tracey's life, someone unexpected, waiting for her to figure out that settling isn't good enough for Tracey *or* her friends?

A romantic comedy bursting with emotion and self-discovery, *The Settle Down Summer* is the story of falling in love, falling out of it, and then tumbling in all over again.

Read Chapter One now!

This bar is not my scene.

But then again, what *is* my scene these days? I look around—well, as best I can under the dim Edison bulbs—and take in the rough wooden floors, the sea shanties written in chalk on the dark blue walls, the high tables surrounded by young men and women wearing clothes much cooler than mine. I can't even describe the fashion, that's how much cooler it is. There was a time when I would have gone nuts for a bar like this. It's the most essential thing about New York City, to a certain group of people, the ones who like to consider themselves young and artistic and rebellious: these barely-lit clubs with their carefully curated playlists.

Now I just feel claustrophobic and dowdy. A winning combination, right? I smile at myself in the mirror behind the rows of artisanal whiskey. And when the hipster bartender thinks I'm smiling at him, I shrug and order a shot of something brown that was distilled just over the bridge. No, not in Brooklyn. In *Queens*. For God's sake! Queens!

He's sliding the drink over the stained bar when a touch jostles my elbow and I jolt forward, *way* more dramatically than necessary. My hand knocks the glass and it tips in slow motion, rolling in a semicircle. Twenty-two dollars in Queens County's finest slides over the bar, collecting loose pennies and a stray peanut.

"Oh, damn." I look helplessly at the bartender. He is giving me what can only be described as the stink-eye. Something tells me there will be no free sympathy refills. I'm pulling out my credit card—I'll just start a tab, and cry over the bill in a month —when someone reaches past me and tosses a card on the bar.

"Put it on my tab," a deep voice growls, cutting through the music, and damn if my heart doesn't flutter a little bit.

My eyes follow the arm up to its owner. There's a man standing next to me—no, not standing. *Looming.* There is a giant of a man looming next to me, his face impossible to read in the twilight of this bar. He's wearing jeans, a dark blue blazer over a blue-checked shirt, and judging by the width of his shoulders, he's the one who jostled my whiskey into oblivion. But since he's paying for it, all is forgiven.

"Hi," I say, and immediately run out of any other words.

The giant turns his attention from the bartender to me, and my breath catches a little. High forehead, short dark hair, a ghost of a five o'clock shadow—this guy has dramatic hero written all over him. And honestly, he's probably not abnormally tall. Maybe six-foot-four? Remember, I'm a shrimp. The view is different from down here.

I see crows-feet crinkle around his eyes as he takes me in. No spring chicken. No problem here. And then he says, "I didn't see you down there."

Of course he does.

Of *course* he does.

"Well, maybe you should pay more attention," I snap. Yes, I'm sensitive about my height. You don't see me going around saying, "Wow, how's the air up there?" to tall people. Teasing someone about their size is about as fair as tormenting a dog because they can't open a door. Nature didn't give them thumbs! What do you want from them?

"I should," he agrees, although maybe he's not as sheepish as I would like. "Let me make it up to you. I'll buy you another."

"No," I say, and give the room a very dramatic scan. Maybe I flip my curls a little. Who can say for sure. "I'm waiting for someone. I'll let him buy it for me."

His presence seems to retreat a little. "I'll leave you alone, then."

And before I know it, he's taking his own whiskey from the bartender and melting away into the crush of people. I find myself watching him, his broad shoulders and height making him an easy target at first. Then he's swallowed up into a crowd near the front of the bar, where the front windows have been pulled wide open, letting the joviality spread onto the street outside.

I turn back to the bartender, who is watching me warily. Probably wants me to get a drink and give up this real estate.

But the guy I'm meeting said to sit at the dead center of the bar. And I don't want to make things hard for him.

"I'll take a whiskey sour," I say, because it will take a few extra seconds to mix, and I've got whiskey on my mind now. The bartender pointedly takes down another expensive bottle, and I guess I should have specified something cheaper, but that's on me. Another Manhattan ritual I've forgotten about.

It feels like I've forgotten *everything* about going out: how to dress, how to put on makeup, how to arrive late so I'm not sitting here being accosted by tall men with handsome faces, how to deal with sharing my space with more people than that occupancy sign can possibly allow.

But that's okay, because I'm about to meet Chase. And Chase is the guy I'm going to settle down with.

* * *

Two Months Earlier

To hear us talking, you'd think we've all just been released from prison—not just three women sitting around drinking wine with our feet drawn up on the sofa cushions.

"We're finally free!"

"I'm *so* ready for hot girl summer!"

"This time, I'm putting it *all* out there!"

"I'm going to put my mouth up against the next hot guy I see on the street."

"Margot!"

We all throw popcorn at Margot, who as usual, is the one who takes things too far.

She laughs and bats it away. In the six years since we moved to New York City together, Margot has only grown more outrageous, more uninhibited, than she'd been back in Iowa. And she'd been considered a *lot* of woman in Iowa, believe me.

A lot more than me. In our years rooming together at Prairie Arts, the prestigious but tiny art school in Iowa where we'd done our degrees, Margot had been a girl you could rely on to start a party anytime, anyplace. I was a girl you could rely on to start a study group.

Everyone said we were perfect together.

But we'd spent ten years and frankly, both of us were starting to wonder when the next phase of our lives would begin.

Summer always seems to shine new light on that question. Maybe it's because in school, we emerged into summer vacation with a sense of real growth. We'd finished something, and we were heading into the future.

Now we were just getting together for the same brunch date we'd had last weekend.

And who knows, maybe the influx of young tourists into the city this time of year—kids on their real summer breaks, grads out on their own for the first time, running wild in this city of unlimited potential for excitement and trouble—makes us remember that feeling.

That huge, gorgeous, what's next feeling.

Whatever it is, in summer, and more emphatically *this* summer, it feels like a decent chunk of the city is just going for broke. In the love and relationships department, for damn sure. It's not just Margot, Caitlyn, and me feeling the pull of summer loving. Manhattan is rocking with hormones and desire, love and relationships, sex and candy.

I see it everywhere I go: people are snogging on the subway, they're going at it in The Ramble, they're hooking up and bumping bits in every stairwell and alley and station from Battery Park City to the Bronx. They're young and they're beautiful and they're free and they're not even looking at me, but I still feel like they're judging me for being almost-thirty and single.

I'm trying not to be crotchety about it, but damn. A woman gets tired of constant sex hanging in the air when she, herself, is not getting any. Can't a woman commute from her Upper West Side apartment to her Union Square gallery without stalking through a fog of pre-, post-, and possibly current coitus?

"You sound like a grandma," Caitlyn laughs.

She's sitting in my favorite armchair—okay, my only armchair, because there is only space for a loveseat and a single chair along the back wall of my living room—with her feet tucked beneath her, long waves of red hair falling over her shoulders. Caitlyn has the smooth skin and confident features of a woman who still believes she will never grow old, only more beautiful. But she's my age, and single again, and I know deep down she's feeling as crotchety as I am.

Her perfect teeth flash as she asks me, "Are you just signing out of sex?"

"Please, I signed out of sex years ago," I retort.

I feel Margot on the loveseat next to me react, her shoulders twitching as she chokes on laughter, but it's no joke. It's *true.* All of us did—even witchy little Margot, with her white-blonde pixie cut and her startling ice-blue eyes. During the pandemic, things got grim for singles with formerly exciting love lives. Some folks we knew ended up hooking up with one another. Some of them got married. A few of them actually moved to the suburbs.

We hadn't done anything like that, but it's beginning to feel like we're the last women standing. Or the last ones on a sinking ship. I nudge Margot until she stops laughing at me as I add, "I don't even know where to sign back in at."

"No, I get you." Caitlyn sips her wine, gazing at a crazy painting of an elephant currently gracing the far wall, next to my living room door.

Well, we *think* it's an elephant. The artist was not forthcoming when I asked. She said it was whatever I wanted it to be. As an art dealer, I know asking the buyer to pretend they had some kind of artistic vision was rarely a useful strategy, so I just tell everyone it's an elephant.

"I *totally* get you," Caitlyn goes on. "I know hook-ups are the hot trend this summer but I'm so over it. I want to go straight to the end, you know? Just me and my husband, dancing at our wedding reception."

"I guess we can wait the summer sex-fest out?" I swirl the wine in my glass. "Maybe the men will be worn out by the end of August and after Labor Day we can interest them in a few nice dinners and a short engagement."

Margot considers the proposition. "It's an idea. I mean, they can't sustain this energy for too long. It's crazy out there. It's like every subway car is someone else's personal strip club, and no one's bringing me a comped drink."

She's not wrong there. The subways are worst of all: the sweaty rush hours packed with laughing, grinning, groping people hanging from the poles, breathing in each other's faces, getting up close and personal with strangers. I usually have a front-row ticket to the show, because I like to sit in a corner seat, even though it can be hard to get out of when the train car gets full and your stop is coming up. I pretend to look at my phone, but all the while I'm feeling like I accidentally wandered into the wrong movie theater.

And the worst part is, I should love the summer shenanigans! The laughing, the grinning, the groping. I try to be jealous. I try to wish I was part of things. But it just isn't my scene. Not anymore. The world shut down, and when I finally ventured outside again, I was older, sadder, and less in the mood for public ass-grabbing than ever.

Caitlyn leans over my coffee table, bottle in hand. "Was that sigh a hint, madam?"

I hold up my glass. "I mean, if you're serving."

As Caitlyn tops me off, I turn to check on Margot, who has been suspiciously quiet. She's thumbing her own glass thoughtfully, gazing out the window. My living room window can have that effect on people. I have the smallest apartment in my circle of friends, *but* I have a view of the Hudson River, and I'd arranged my small sofa and armchair so that everyone in the room can see out. Having a great view is better than TV in this town.

We'd had one of those rich blue summer dusks tonight, and now lights twinkle alluringly in the distance. Even if they're just the New Jersey skyline, those glowing lights have a way of reminding a person they're in magical, mythical Manhattan. A way of making a person feel good. We are in New York City and we are *making it*—how many people can say that?

That's how those lights *used* to make me feel, anyway—every day and every night. Now they just made me feel lonesome, like I am on a lonely island in a sea of humanity. The part of me which loves this town withered to a few barren branches over the past few years, and now every day is a struggle.

But I'm trying to flourish here again. I really am. I don't *really* want to move to the suburbs.

I don't think.

Caitlyn waves the chardonnay bottle in Margot's direction, trying to get her attention. She'd be wise to ignore Caitlyn. By tomorrow morning, we'll all regret drinking this stuff—it's cheap, awful, girl's-night-out wine, sweet and cloying as peach nectar. But I had three bottles left over from a low-key gallery opening I hosted last night, and none of us are doing *so* great that we can say no to free wine.

Margot doesn't look up. It's like she's lost in her thoughts, and not even the prospect of a refill is enough to get her back.

Caitlyn gives me a head-shake that says, *Here we go again.*

I shrug and toy with my short cap of chocolate-colored curls, absently looping them around my fingers the way I've been doing since I was a toddler. What can we do but wait Margot out? If she's dreaming up one of her new schemes, all we can do is watch the show and applaud when it's over.

I decide to keep our conversation going, let Margot do whatever brainstorming she needs over there. "So yeah, today was the craziest day yet. There was practically an orgy on the D train. I got off at 34th Street and walked to the gallery."

Caitlyn lifts her eyebrows appreciatively. "I *thought* your calves were looking hot. I was guessing Stairmaster."

"Twenty blocks in heels, actually." I look down at my feet, flexing them. "I still don't have it in me to go near a gym."

"I hear that." Caitlyn tucks in her stomach, patting what she assumes is excess. If anything, she has gone from a size four to an eight in the past two years. Hardly unhealthy for a woman of her height, but I can understand that is its own trauma. And she's been going through it. Caitlyn's occasional work in TV production has slowly dried up and she's been devoting herself to her hobby, which is the weather. She developed a website for armchair meteorologists like herself, but she was the first to admit sitting at a desk coding was nothing like running around hot sets all day. "I was hoping shut-in weight would be sexy," she says morosely.

"That's another thing. All those beautiful young things out there—how do they all stay so skinny?"

"Easy," Caitlyn sighs. "They *don't* stay home like we do. Also: youthful metabolisms."

The wine is sticky on my tongue. I drink more anyway, because there's nothing else to do and I'm certainly not going to stick this bottle back in the fridge, save it for later. "I was looking forward to getting back out there this year," I confess. "But now I just feel like I'm just a bystander to everyone else's smoking-hot summer."

"Well, you're old," Caitlyn informs me with a wry grin. "We all are. It's okay to admit it. You wanna go up on the roof and yell at clouds? Should be some gorgeous high cirrus out there tonight."

"I can't." I stretch out my toes. "My feet hurt too much from walking twenty blocks in heels."

There was a time when that walk wouldn't have left me sore from my hips to my arches. But my commute went from daily to biweekly back when the city was shut down, and now my gallery is almost solely run out of my tiny living room. I only go downtown for special showings.

At home, I change out artwork piece by piece on my best-lit wall, take quality photos, and put those on my gallery website. When buyers want to see something in person, I wrap the work up, take a car service downtown, and set up the gallery for their visit. I've been thinking of reinstating regular hours, allowing walk-ins, but my customer base has shifted online and it seems like too much trouble.

Also, I have to wear heels when I'm at the gallery, and once you *stop* wearing heels, it seems very hard to get back into them.

And yes, I really have to totter around in high heels. I'm *really* short. It's no joke when you're trying to sell a big statement piece to a man almost two feet taller than you are. Well, it's a joke to him. "That painting's bigger than you are!" he says.

All of them say it.

"I'm going to quit wearing heels," I say, testing the idea.

Caitlyn flexes her own beautiful toes at me. "You can't give up heels yet. That's the first step towards just plain giving up."

"Well, maybe it's time. I mean, look outside, Caitlyn. The city came back to life and it's ten years younger than we are. Everyone out there is an infant. We're the old ones now."

"Define old!"

"Do *you* want to hook up with a random guy you ran into on the D train?"

She wrinkles her perfect nose at me. "Eww, no."

"But you have before, right?"

"Yes, *but,* in my defense, that was the *L* train, and it was also six years ago—"

"Precisely my point. Six years ago."

We look at each for a moment. Comprehension is dawning on Caitlyn's face. "We can't keep up," she says slowly. "And I don't even *want* to keep up. Tracey, when did we get old?"

There's a moment of stunned silence while we take in the fatal shot of that word. *Old.* It means different things in different societies. In New York City, it generally means anyone over twenty-seven. Even that number might be a high estimate. It takes stamina to live and work and love in this city. You need a lot of energy. You need a lot of energy *drinks*—which make me sick, unfortunately. But the point is, everything takes everything in this town. Careers. Errands. Socializing. *Dating.* We've seen friends give it all up, shake their heads, say the city is a young person's game.

Are we next?

Margot puts down her wine glass with a startling *clink* on my tiny coffee table. She turns to us with a bright smile on her pixie face. We wait for her proclamation with interest. Margot is our dreamer. Margot is our woman of ideas. Whatever she says will be interesting and inspiring and probably knock us right out of this funk we've just found ourselves in.

She claps her hands, the same move she used to use on her little students back when she first moved to the city and taught art at a fancy FiDi school. "It's time to settle down, girls!"

That's...not what I expected. Not from Margot, anyway.

Looking across the sofa, I see Caitlyn is equally confused. She runs a hand over her face, as if trying to clear her mind for this. For whatever Margot really means. "Settle down, like, how? Like time we start that commune?"

About four years ago, we talked about buying a Victorian house in Ditmas Park, Brooklyn and starting our own commune. It was a bad break-up thing. Ultimately we couldn't get financing and then Caitlyn met a guy and Margot met a girl and I launched my own gallery and the idea got left on the wayside. But there were a few points over the past few years when I really wished we were all weathering the storms together in a big old house with stained glass accents, rather than in three small one-bedroom apartments scattered around Manhattan.

"*Not* a commune. The opposite of that, actually." Margot's smile is a serene bow, cherry-red and twice as sweet. "We're going to get married and move out of the city."

I can feel my eyebrows lifting into my scalp. "I don't think all three of us can get married. We have to pick one couple, and then the last person will have to be our very special friend."

"I'm not the extra in this scenario," Caitlyn warned. "Don't even try it. I'm legal or nothing."

"You guys." Margot shakes her head, her white-blonde hair falling over her eyes. She looks like a mischievous fairy. "No. We won't marry each other, although that's charming and I love that your minds went there first. But that's not what we want. Or what we need. I'm talking a regular, ho-hum, everyday marriage."

We look at each other, then back at Margot. "Is that what we need?" I ask, skeptical.

"It's exactly what we need," Margot assures me. "Peace. Stability. And *space.* This is the summer that we settle down, get married, and move to the suburbs. Or at least a glorious three-bedroom in Queens. Don't you want that?"

She stands up, reaching her hands out from side to side. I know the point she's going to make before she even does it, before she tilts her body to the left, leaning over with the litheness of many years of yoga, until her left hand hits the wall. Then she straightens, and does the same thing to the wall on her right.

Yes, my living room is small. But that's part of all this, right? Touching both walls of your living room without having to move your feet—that's part of living the dream, being a New Yorker. So is being stir-crazy, wishing you had a three-bedroom in Fort Lee like your old friend Liv, staying up late scrolling Zillow with "Must Have Pool" checked. It's all part of the lifestyle. Wouldn't trade it for the world. Don't look at my search history.

I shake my head. "Margot, you have a lot of ideas, but this one is without a doubt your craziest."

She is still leaning against the wall, her petite frame tilted at a 45-degree angle. "Is it? Caitlyn? What do you think? Time to get married and make the next step?"

Caitlyn has tilted back her glass and is draining it of tragic white wine. After the last gulp is gone, she looks over at me and shrugs. "You know, I think she's right."

I can't stop myself from blinking a few times. Margot is the dreamer of our group, the one who blames everything on Mercury in retrograde, the one who wore cowboy boots with a ballgown to a black-tie gala, the one who once spent a weekend starting a vineyard on a roof in Red Hook.

But Caitlyn is the realist among us. And she is not afraid to own that title. She went on record telling Margot that teeny-tiny planet next to the sun was not causing her bathroom sink to drip all night; she warned Margot that going off-script at the gala would get her in trouble with her boss; she suggested that Margot not sink every last dime of her savings into a bunch of vines on top of a six-story building.

Margot laughed her off every time, but she also didn't get a decent night's sleep for two weeks before she finally got her sink fixed; she landed in the doghouse at her job for wearing those boots and missed a promotion over it; she lost her investment three months into the vineyard when a hurricane blew through the city, taking out her precious vines in what the insurance company callously named an "Act of God" which they couldn't be responsible for.

We don't like to say Caitlyn is always right, but we all know Caitlyn is always right.

Me, by the way? They call me the mom of the group. This is not a compliment to me, but they think it is. I see myself as a helper to my talented friends. I am kind of artistic—hence the gallery I run. But I am also kind of ordinary—hence it's not *my* art gracing the gallery walls.

I'm very average. It took me a while to learn that, but now I consider this kind of self-knowledge one of my strengths.

Margot has straightened up; she walks over to the living room window and flings it open. The sounds of the city flood in: sirens, car horns, a jet on approach to LaGuardia, an Amtrak train rumbling north in its tunnel along the Hudson, a woman laughing from another building's tiny courtyard. For years this was a symphony to my ears. There were times when just hearing the city out there meant we were all alive, we would all make it. It was a comfort.

The noise feels intrusive now, like I got used to the silence and I want it back. I remember days when I could leave that window open and just hear the odd barking dog, the occasional siren. Days when the rattle of leaves from the spindly courtyard trees seemed to be a song all their own. These are the sounds of the suburbs, and I know it, and I want them back with an intensity that makes me wonder who I even am anymore.

Margot closes the window, shutting out the din. "I'm done with it. I'm ready to write my *Goodbye to All That*. Aren't you? Don't you want to just wash your hands of this city, of this madness? I always meant to have four kids, you know. Where will I ever put them in this town?"

"You're saying we should jump ship," Caitlyn says. "Leave the city to the strong. For we are weak. Is that it?"

"Leave the city to the *young*," Margot corrects her. "Let's get out. Let's allow the kids to grind on the subway in peace. Let's be good to our feet and stop commuting in heels. Let's buy houses and have yards and raise kids and maybe get some of those backyard chickens everyone loves so much. No roosters, though."

"How are we going to do all this, if it's not a commune?" I ask. "I certainly can't finance a house on my own. And, guys, I love you, but I am one hundred percent hetero. So marriage is still off the table."

"Oh, we'll get married," Margot says. "All three of us. Not to each other, though. If we put all our effort into it, and look in the right places, we'll find husbands in no time. I guarantee it."

"Why does this sound like a pyramid scheme?" Caitlyn asks. "How many boxes do you have in your apartment right now? What happens to you if you don't get enough members to sign up?"

"This is not a pyramid scheme. This is just a plain old scheme." Margot's glacier-blue eyes are glittering with excitement, and I feel myself leaning forward, absorbing her craziness into my own body. "A house! A yard! Kids! A dog! A cat! Chickens!"

"A Lexus!" Caitlyn adds. "A home office that isn't also my bedroom!"

"A husband," Margot announces gleefully. "Out mowing the yard, getting all sweaty, jumping in the pool, calling you to hop in with him—"

The fantasy is getting more vivid by the moment.

Let's do it, I think feverishly. *What could be worse than what we've already got?*

"Let's get married!" I leap to my feet, spilling my wine across the floor. The dry old floorboards thirstily drink it up. "Let's settle down!"

Margot takes my hands and we do a quick, thrilling dance around the room which ends when she bumps into my TV table, nearly sending the flatscreen crashing to the floor. "Let's buy houses where there's enough room to dance," she teases, straightening the TV.

Find The Settle Down Summer at nataliekreinert.shop, or your favorite book retailer.

Acknowledgments

THIS SERIES HAS been two years in the making...or maybe more, I'm not even sure anymore. I wrote the first drafts in a big rush, then simply ran out of time and energy to figure out how I wanted to market them. As an equestrian fiction writer first, and romance writer second, I wasn't sure my readers would want them. But quite a few assured me they did, especially everyone in my Patreon!

So as always, let me thank my incredible Patreon subscribers...and if you want to join them, here are my subscriptions:

Find subscription opportunities at patreon.com/nataliekreinert, reamstories.com/nataliekreinert, or, for my theme park fans, imaginarymemories.substack.com.

My subscribers include: Ashley Swink, Eris, Jocelyn Bissett, Erika Thomas, Shelby Graft, Nicole Russo, Karen Wolfsheimer, Pamela Allen-LeBlanc, Raina Kujawa, Kellie Halteman, Jennifer Williams, Natalie Clark, Megan McDonald, Adrienne

Brant, Sally Testa, Becca B., April Lutz, Julia Koeger, Heidi Schmid, Mel Sperti, Cathy Luo, Elana Rabinow, Laura, Empathy, Tayla Travella, Gretchen Fieser, JoAnn Flejszar, Nancy Neid, Libby Henderson, Maureen VanDerStad, Sherron Meinert, Leslie Yazurlo, Nicola Beisel, Mel Policicchio, Harry Burgh, Kylie Standish, Kathlynn Angie-Buss, Peggy Dvorsky, Christine Komis, Thoma Jolette Parker, Karen Carrubba, Emma Gooden, Katie Lewis, Silvana Ricapito, Sarine Laurin, Di Hannel, Jennifer, Claus Giloi, Heather Walker, Cyndy Searfoss, Kaylee Amons, Mary Vargas, Kathi Lacasse, Rachael Rosenthal, Orpu, Diana Aitch, Liz Greene, Zoe Bills, Cheryl Bavister, Sarah Seavey, Tricia Jordan, Brinn Dimler, Lindsay Moore, Rhonda Lane, C Sperry, Heather Voltz, Kim Keller, Renee Knowles, Annika Kostrabula, Alyssa, Susan Lambiris, Shauna, Lisa Heck, Dianna, SailorEpona, Megan Devine, and Michelle Beck!

Thanks so much, lovely people!

About the Author

I LIVE ON a small farm in Florida, and when I'm not writing, I'm usually gardening or playing with my horses. I've spent most of my life as an equestrian, including several years as a member of the NYC Parks Department's mounted unit along with a few more non-horsey years in the city.

Visit my website at nataliekreinert.com to keep up with the latest news and read occasional blog posts and book reviews. For previews, installments of upcoming fiction, and exclusive stories, visit my Patreon page at patreon.com/nataliekreinert and learn how you can become one of my team members. For more, find me on social media:

Reader Group: facebook.com/groups/nataliesreaders

Instagram: instagram.com/nataliekreinert

Join my email list for exclusive offers and news at nataliekreinert.shop

Email: natalie@nataliekreinert.com

Made in the USA
Columbia, SC
24 September 2023

23187293R00112